THE NECROMOUSER AND OTHER MAGICAL CATS

MARY E. LOWD

For Lane and Lee

With special thanks to Ursula K. Le Guin and James Howe for Catwings and Bunnicula.

CONTENTS

PART I

THE NECROMOUSER

1

THE NECROMOUSER

SHREDDY NEVER HAD a particular taste for fish, but he'd been in a sour mood for days.

The Red-Haired Woman had won their latest skirmish over the orchids. She'd cordoned off the kitchen window with chicken wire. Shreddy rattled the wire, pulling with his claws at the edges. He shoved his face into the few centimeters between wire and wall, wrinkling his nose and squinting his eyes at the discomfort, but the wire didn't have enough give. Shreddy couldn't get his head through.

As the days passed, the orchids flourished and basked in their new protection. Without suffering chewed leaves and frequent up-rootings, they began putting forth lush purple blooms. Shreddy was infuriated. The perfect promise-shaped buds mocked him, and the delicate spots on their tentatively opening petals made him seethe inside.

On the one week anniversary of the Day of the Chicken Wire, Shreddy skulked through the house slashing furniture and knocking petty objects, like pens and paperclips, off the Red-Haired Woman's desk. But that wasn't enough.

Shreddy was a fat tabby who never cared for mice, or

birds, or fish. He liked catnip toys and colorful ribbons; his favorite toy was a Koosh ball on a string. The Red-Haired Woman dangled it for him, and that was the way it should be. So, he didn't attack the goldfish for his own benefit. No, he would have preferred to leave the goldfish alone. Yes, the Red-Haired Woman forced him into it. And it was extremely distasteful. He watched the gasping fish flop on the floor, and he struck it a few times with his paw to make it stop.

There. That would teach her. Shreddy stretched out on the floor, feeling better.

That would have been the end of it if his whimsical cat-mind hadn't happened on the perfect cherry to top off his sundae of rebellion. He would hide the fish, somewhere inconvenient, for the Red-Haired Woman to find it later.

He took the slimy, dead object in his mouth, curling his lips away from the scaly flesh. Fate provided the perfect place—a broken *All-in-One*. Shreddy dropped the fish in the empty paper slot for feeding paper through, an indentation deep enough to completely obscure the tiny body; then he stretched out, pleased with himself, on the device's control panel. The weight of his stripey girth pressed down the "start" buttons for faxing, scanning, printing... everything the All-in-One could do.

Before the orchids and before the All-in-One broke, the behemoth machine had been the primary source of contention between Shreddy and the Red-Haired Woman.

Against the Woman's wishes, Shreddy liked to sleep on the control panel of the All-in-One. "Shroedinger!" she would shriek, shooing him off, and he would do his best to ignore her. Nonetheless, it had made his ears twitch and twist around backward when his weight inevitably turned the machine on, inspiring mechanical whirrings, electrical hummings, and sometimes a glowing green light. Shreddy liked the All-in-One much better now it was broken.

To Shreddy's great distress on this day of the Brutally Murdered Fish, the All-in-One leapt to life underneath him. He flattened his ears, trying not to hear the hummings and whirrings under his body, but they vibrated through him, echoing louder in his ears than they ever had before. When the green light flashed, it filled his eyes with ghostly after-image. Shreddy feared it had blinded him. His paws felt weak and unreal to him, but he leapt off the machine, panting like a puppy. It was as if his contact with the machine had electrically shocked him. He would know better than to sleep on a broken All-in-One again.

Then, as his vision cleared, Shreddy saw movement in the paper feeder. A tiny gold fin was flapping, and, as Shreddy watched, the once-dead gold fish flopped its way out of the All-in-One. Shreddy tilted his head, looking at the fish quizzically. He had felt its cold, limp, body in his mouth. No heart had beaten in the tiny, scaled breast.

The All-in-One powered down, kachunking its internal moving pieces back to their rest states. Had the All-in-One resurrected the goldfish?

Shreddy looked back at the gasping fish, dying once again on the floor. As the fish drew its last strained breath, Shreddy felt his own chest constrict. For an instant, he saw through the goldfish's eyes. How terrible to die as a fish! He would have to find a new place to hide it. More importantly, Shreddy decided he would have to find a more useful beast to test the All-in-One's powers on. If that machine could help him raise the dead—and possibly channel his mind into the resurrected corpses, using them as his minions—it would give him Great Power.

It would give him the power to fit *through* the chicken wire... He *had* to find out.

Shreddy was not a hunter, but he devoted the rest of the week to tracking and attacking mice. The Red-Haired Woman had never been happier with him, but he was unable to enjoy her praises. He daily worried that she would throw the broken All-in-One away. He had to hurry.

The first three mice were a disaster. After resurrection, despite Shreddy's immense concentration, each of them scurried away. In his fazed, drained state brought on by the noise and lights of the All-in-One, Shreddy was unable to recapture the raised mice or take control of them. He experienced a strange dual existence, each time, until the mouse re-died. This didn't take long, since the mice were generally quite panicked by their experience being captured by Shreddy, not to mention deeply confused by the metaphysical experience of dying and resurrecting as part cat.

Shreddy lay on the floor, eyes dilated and ears flattened, viscerally experiencing a mad dash through the ductwork or the unpleasantness of being caught by another cat, once back outside. He hoped his attacks to the brainless beasts were equally frightening. They certainly deserved it for what they were putting him through.

On the fourth mouse, Shreddy had a stroke of luck. Although, it was a mixed blessing. Losing his patience with the tedium of catching mice, Shreddy had taken his aggression out on his soon-to-be host: the mouse's back legs were broken, completely crushed by Shreddy's horrific (and splendorous) mauling.

Since the mouse couldn't run away, Shreddy was able to properly focus on it and take the time he needed to learn dominion over his tiny, pained minion. However, Shreddy couldn't take the pain for long—as he controlled the mouse, practicing using its body, he experienced the excruciating pain it felt in its broken limbs. Shreddy put the miserable beast out of its misery. Out of *his* misery. He would be able to use the next mouse properly. The taste of orchid greens was nearly his again. He could almost feel the fleshy plants between his teeth.

Mouse number five proved harder to control. Although Shreddy could see through its eyes and shared partial control of its body, the mouse proved to have a mind of its own! Shreddy had to smack it down, dizzyingly, with his paw. Dealing and receiving the same claw-filled blow stretched his perception of reality in a mind-blowing way. He was walking on both sides of the thin line dividing pleasure and pain. Unfortunately, the mouse re-died during the momentous experience. Shreddy deftly resurrected it again, making mouse number five also mouse number six.

After a quick repeat of the same interchange, mouse numbers five and six also became mouse number seven. The mouse, who Shreddy had come to think of as "Orchidbane," was much more pliable to Shreddy's control after its third death and resurrection. Fortunately, Shreddy had remembered to treat the mouse carefully while killing it, and Orchidband was still in good (albeit less than mint) condition.

Shreddy spent the rest of the afternoon curled up in the kitchen sink, resting after his valiant struggle. He left Orchidbane quivering in the All-in-One.

As Shreddy fell heavily into the abysses of sleep, he dragged Orchidbane with him. Their dreams mingled. The hunter was hunted, and the hunted was horrified by his power. The smell of cheese wafted through the dual dreams, both delighting and disgusting them. When nightmare phantoms reared, their instincts conflicted: fight *and* flight, they said.

Shreddy awoke less rested than when he'd fallen asleep. It was time to get this job done. He stalked back to the All-in-One, where he extracted Orchidbane from the paper feeder. Delicately, he carried himself (well, his mouse-form) inside his own mouth. It was warm and wet inside. He leapt lightly to the kitchen counter and placed the mouse under the windowsill. It was an easy jump for a cat from counter to sill, but Orchidbane had to scramble up Shreddy's back, using the cat as a ladder to reach the height of the offending chicken wire. Shreddy's brain felt like it did a back flip trying to understand the sensation that mouse paws on a cat back—all controlled by the same mind—created.

Shreddy watched intently with his own cat eyes as his Orchidbane body squeezed through one of the holes in the chicken wire. Nose twitching, Orchidbane skittered across the windowsill and up to the first orchid pot. With a little leap, he landed in the moist potting soil. He sunk his claws into the base of the lush orchid stem (Shreddy gave a sigh of contentment) and stared up the length of the flower. Orchids were trees to him.

One by one, Orchidbane climbed the orchids until they drooped downward, eventually breaking their stalks. Then, biting deep into the green flesh (another catly sigh with each bite—who knew orchid's would taste as sweet to mouse teeth?), he dragged the orchids, flower end first, toward and through the chicken wire. Pulling the flowers through the inch-wide wire holes stripped their leaves and mangled them. Shreddy didn't care. Once his faithful mouse was done, Shreddy feasted on them. He gnawed the stalks until they became white and stringy. He batted the misused blooms about, chasing them from end to end of the linoleum kitchen floor. He sated himself after his long and unwillingly endured abstinence from orchids.

The Red-Haired Woman returned from her day at work to find Shreddy deep asleep, wound in orchids. The mouse, Orchidbane, had been abandoned, carelessly, in a stupor on the counter. The Woman shrieked when she saw him—both Shreddy and the mouse—but, she would have been hard-pressed to decide which distressed her more: destroyed orchids or vermin in her kitchen? Shreddy slept better after the mouse was destroyed. His brain was washed clean by pure, feline dreams.

Blinking his eyes, Shreddy roused to the world slowly the next morning. It was uncatly of him to sleep the whole night through, never rearranging himself to find better comfort or moving from spot to spot, as if sampling the quality of sleep in each. Yesterday's antics had drained him, and so he had slept the sleep of the dead.

The orchid remains were gone. He noticed that first. Then he realized the chicken wire had been removed. He leapt into the window to enjoy his hard earned right. It should have been his simply by nature of his cathood. Cats own window sills.

Yet, something was missing. His triumph should have been complete...

Suddenly, Shreddy felt the diminished state of his existence. Where he had lived in two bodies, he now lived in one. The Red-Haired Woman had killed his other self! No matter. He would make another self. Perhaps he would make two and live a threefold life. Or four? His eyes dilated, possessively, as he thought of the possibilities. He felt the urge to sleep on the All-in-One while he planned his nefarious deeds.

Unfortunately, during the night, Shreddy's fears had

been realized. The Red-Haired Woman had moved the All-in-One out to the curb with the trash and recycling. When he found it there, his heart was nearly broken. It was as if the Red-Haired Woman were trying to kill the tiny parts of him that were yet to be born. He would have to hurry before the garbage truck came. He would kill and resurrect as many mice as he could. (The idea made his head spin.) No! He would resurrect a bird and feel what it's like to fly!

Frantically, Shreddy climbed the cherry tree in the front yard and crouched in its crotch. He waited impatiently for birds to fly by, and when they did he leapt haphazardly at them, paws flailing. By sheer luck and the element of surprise, he managed to knock a sparrow out of the air. Although, he fell awkwardly from the tree with it.

Despite the urban myth, cats don't always land on their feet. Especially if they are overweight and careless.

Shreddy recovered, but the bird didn't. He carried it, lovingly, possessively, in his mouth. He trotted, quickly, toward the soon to be discarded All-in-One. His ears flattened as he heard the garbage truck turn onto the end of the block and begin toddling its way up the street. *Hurry.* There would only be time for one last minion, but he would learn to *fly.* (His stomach twisted at the idea, but there was no time to be queasy.)

Three more houses, and the truck would be here. Shreddy stuffed the bird in the paper feeder, and bounced onto the control panel. His stomach lurched in preparation for the leeching sensation as his mind was funneled into the re-rousing bird.

It didn't happen. (Two more houses.)

Shreddy jumped off and on again, slamming the control panel with all his portly weight. Nothing. (One more house.) He batted his paw against the large green buttons. *Nothing.*

The garbage truck parked in front of the Red-Haired Woman's house. The garbage man swung off of the back of the truck and lifted the trash can, deftly emptying it into the back of the truck.

Shreddy crouched possessively on his All-in-One, but the garbage man shooed him away. Shreddy had to relinquish his beloved electronic box. He watched the power of his necromancy crash into the pile of common rubbish.

As the truck and All-in-One pulled away, Shreddy counted up his little minions in his mind: one fish, three mice that ran away, one mouse with broken legs, and three resurrections for Orchidbane. Eight. And one life of his own. Nine.

Of course he couldn't raise the sparrow, *not without sacrificing himself*. He didn't notice the unplugged power cord, hanging uselessly, out of the back of the garbage truck driving away.

That evening, the Red-Haired Woman greeted Shreddy warmly. "I don't know how you did it," she said, "but chicken wire won't do me any good if you can pull my orchids through it." She was carrying a new potted plant, which she set in the kitchen window. She had bought a catnip plant to replace her orchids.

2

SHREDDY AND THE ZOMB-DOGS

WHEN SHREDDY WAS A YOUNG CAT, he and the red-haired woman lived alone. Shreddy enjoyed his youth and, in later years, he often daydreamed of those days before the red-haired woman declared: "I think I'll take up a hobby."

Shreddy wasn't worried at the time. She'd taken up a hobby before, growing orchids, and he'd found her pastime perfectly delightful. Delectable, even. This time, the red-haired woman decided to grow something that Shreddy couldn't eat.

"Isn't she adorable?" the red-haired woman asked Shreddy. He fluffed his fur and bared his claws, but the red-haired woman didn't notice. "I hope you two will be friends."

Shreddy didn't think so. Shreddy thought he would slash the cuddly, little, speckled brown and white Cavalier King Charles Spaniel right across the nose. *That*, however, the red-haired woman noticed, but it was worth it. Susie, the speckled spaniel, knew from day one to give Shreddy his space.

Susie wouldn't have been so bad, but Shreddy hated it every time she had puppies. Each litter was two months of hell. Worse, sometimes not all of the puppies sold right away. Invariably, it would be Shreddy's least favorite of the sniveling, whining, icky little creatures that stuck around for the extra month. Or half year. *Shudder.* Shreddy didn't understand why anyone bought the little brats at all. But he was glad when they did.

Susie whined and cried whenever the last puppy from one of her litters was finally sold. Shreddy sniggered. He wasn't completely heartless though. Whenever Susie *lost* a puppy, even Shreddy stood at attention in the window watching the somber proceedings of the little funerals outside. He may have hated the little brats, but cats understand the seriousness of death.

Over the years, the little row of tombstones in the garden grew. Five were stillborns; one had a weak heart; and two were too adventurous with necks too weak for their own good. Shreddy mourned them all. Though, he would have *hated* them had they lived.

It was an unhappy equilibrium, for Shreddy, but it was stable. Puppies came, and puppies would go. Grumpy cats will be grumpy. All might have been well, if the red-haired-woman could have left well enough alone.

Shreddy, Susie, and their shared master.

But then...

It was Shreddy, Susie, *Cooper*, and a woman who Shreddy would no longer acknowledge.

Cooper was a yellow, toy Labradoodle. Where Susie looked like a painfully precious pillow-decoration, Cooper looked and acted more like a mop. Nothing could be more contemptible. Susie, however, was smitten, giving Shreddy one more reason to despise her. That reason multiplied the next time—and every subsequent time—she bore a litter of puppies.

As if Susie's puppies had not been contemptible enough before, they now sported Cooper's ridiculous blonde curls and idiotic grin. Whole litterfuls of *Cooper*.

Shreddy had to take action, and a few weeks after the second litter of abominations was completely sold, Shreddy came up with the perfect plan.

"COOPER," he purred, ingratiatingly one day. "Have you seen that magic, shiny box that the red-haired woman adores?"

Cooper was busy shoving his head under various couch cushions for no apparent reason, so it took him a moment to respond. And, when he did, his voice was slightly muffled. "Yeah," he barked, "What of it?"

Shreddy suppressed his inherent desire to yowl, "*What are you doing, you stupid dog!*" at Cooper and instead launched into an insidious, complex, and logically self-contradictory (but Cooper would never realize that) discussion of how the red-haired woman clearly loved her magic, shiny box more than she loved Cooper.

By the time Shreddy was done talking, Cooper's couch-mangling activities had slowed to a halt. He was unusually still for his hyperactive Labradoodle self. It looked like he was actually trying out thinking. Shreddy didn't think the experiment was going so well for him.

"If I were you," Shreddy offered, "I'd bury the horrible thing. In the yard somewhere. *If I were you.*" He sounded immensely casual and looked like he was more interested in cleaning his claws than talking to Cooper. Which wasn't entirely untrue. Nevertheless, Shreddy was extremely gratified when Cooper wandered off muttering about whether magic boxes had a scent and wondering whether they were trackable by nose. Step one was well underway.

As the day wore on, Shreddy's self-satisfied notions turned to glowering. He *liked* the red-haired woman's smartphone. He'd spent many happy evenings sitting on her shoulder, watching the little lurching and zooming figures on the shiny screen as she played her favorite app, *Cars Vs. Zombies.* Sometimes, he'd even reach out a paw and try to catch them.

The red-haired woman had let him play once... When he'd finally gotten his paws on them, the little figures were invisible to the touch. But he could see them skittering!

Shreddy grumbled. He hoped Cooper didn't find the phone.

But Cooper did. And he buried it in the garden. Among the tombstones.

Shreddy shuddered at the sacrilegious desecration as he watched Cooper, nose-down in the dirt, from the safety of the window. *Nevermind*, he thought, *I'll get the phone back. Step two. I'll wait a few days, and when the woman is frantic, I'll tell Cooper to lead her to the phone.*

Cooper would think he was the heroic rescuer, but the red-haired woman would see him for what he truly was: a wretch who dug in her garden and stole her phone. And that would be the end of Cooper.

Perhaps it might have worked, if not for the lightning.

But that night, after the red-haired woman gave up searching for her phone and went to bed and Shreddy lay twitching beside her, dreaming of playing *Cars Vs. Zombies*, there was a lightning storm of awesome proportion. Winds and rain rioted the air, and lightening forked across the sky followed by the hideous crack of thunder... and the crack of an elm branch, thick as the telephone pole it crashed into.

The elm branch tumbled, tangled in telephone and power lines, down to the garden beneath. Angry, urgent electrons coursed from the broken ends of those lines, desperately seeking the lower ground offered by the garden.

Inside the house, Shreddy and the red-haired woman slept fitfully; Cooper slept soundly; and, Susie awoke suddenly. She knew, deep inside her, that something was wrong. Whining and tucking her tail worriedly between her hind legs, Susie risked the storm and took the pet door outside. Peering through the dark, she looked at the garden, but her dog's eyes couldn't see a thing.

"Shreddy!" she woofed. "Shreddy! Shreddy!" Running back inside, she roused the angry cat and begged him to come with her, lending his night vision to her cause. Normally, Shreddy would have spat at her and slashed her nose for waking him. Tonight...

Shreddy came outside. Glowing eyes looked into the night, and what Shreddy saw made his fur stand straight on end.

Puppies rose from their graves.

Lurching, decomposing, horrible puppies. Covered in dirt clods. In various stages of decomposition. "We have to re-kill them," Shreddy whispered to himself. They looked like squished bugs. Only worse. Shreddy knew they had to die.

Then he looked at Susie, her night-blind eyes staring blankly at him. She implored him with a whimper-whine. *"What do you see?"*

"Nothing," Shreddy said, realizing that the mother of these undead monstrosities could be no help to him. She'd fall apart the instant she saw her darling babies hideously reanimated. No, she must be protected against ever discovering what the night's dark shielded her from.

The puppies were approaching. "Go inside," Shreddy hissed urgently. "Guard the woman. Don't leave her side all night. She needs your protection." That would get rid of Susie. Now, though it pained Shreddy to say it, he knew he would need help: "But wake Cooper, and send him to me."

Cooper might be an idiot, but he was stronger than Shreddy.

While Shreddy waited, he watched the activity in the garden. The horrifying little zombie dogs were nuzzling around, woofing and yipping, "Brains! Brains!", from their decaying jaws. Just like the little figures in *Cars Vs. Zombies*, only canine and real.

"What's up?" Cooper said when he arrived.

"Zombies," Shreddy explained. And as he said it, he realized: he knew how to kill zombies. *With cars.* "We need to steal a car." To Shreddy's consternation, cars in the real world didn't start as soon as he lightly set a paw on them. Apparently, video games could be misleading. Undaunted, Shreddy directed Cooper to find a large branch and, with it grasped firmly in his mouth, Cooper bludgeoned away at the windows of the car. Shreddy had seen people sitting inside cars, so he *knew* if he could just get inside, the car would obligingly zoom away and smash down zombies. That's what cars did. *Only he couldn't get inside.*

Frustrated and grumbling, Shreddy wanted to give up on the whole project and get a good night of sleep in the plushy orange chair. How bad could a few zomb-pups living in the backyard really be? Then he saw two things that changed his mind.

First, against all odds, the puppies caught a mouse. The poor thing must have let curiosity get the better of her...

There was no way the blundering zomb-pups could have caught her if she'd been smart enough to keep away. "Argh! Brains!" she squeaked, limping about, freshly turned by the zomb-pups. It was the most horrible, icky waste of a plump, tasty mouse that Shreddy had ever seen.

Then, second and much more upsetting, Cooper ran into his friend Buster, another neighborhood dog. Buster had been dead for nearly three months. He was a boxer mix. Twice the height and weight of Cooper. Which meant the zombie problem was more serious and farther reaching than Shreddy had realized.

"There's something wrong with Buster," Cooper confided to Shreddy after the two of them safely evaded the large, lumbering zomb-dog by ducking under the front porch and escaping through the back.

Buster was too large—and stupid—to follow them.

"He's a *zombie*," Shreddy hissed. "And I don't know how to kill him."

"Is that why we were messing with the car?" Cooper asked settling into a crouch behind Shreddy who was peering gingerly around the corner of the house. "'Cause bashing cars with sticks is no way to kill things."

Shreddy turned his glowing night gaze full on Cooper. *Did this dog have an idea?*

"If you want to kill something," Cooper said, "you bash it with a stick. Not something else." Cooper snorted, clearly tickled with his own cleverness.

Shreddy flexed his claws, and his eyes narrowed to angry slits. After seeing Cooper's success with the window, Shreddy was not optimistic about his chances against moving targets. He was reminded of exactly why he'd decided he was willing to sacrifice the red-haired woman's smartphone to get rid of Cooper. Clearly it had been a bad trade: Cooper was still here, and Shreddy was hunting real zombies in the cold and dark instead of watching the red-haired woman smoosh e-zombies on a comfy couch.

"Cooper," Shreddy said, measuring out his words carefully before saying them, "It's time to bring back that magic box you buried."

"The one the red-haired woman loves better than me? Why would I do that?"

"You'll be a hero," Shreddy answered, but what he was really thinking was, *You'll be a zombie.* To fetch the smartphone from where it was buried in the garden, Cooper would have to go nose-down in the dirt, right in the middle of zombie-central. Shreddy felt extremely evil as he said, "The red-haired woman will be so grateful. She'll probably give you bacon." Being evil was so *easy.* And thrilling.

Cooper fell for it, and Shreddy felt all the hairs along his spine rise in a plume as he watched the foolish Labradoodle obliviously trot into the garden and begin digging. The dirt flew up around his Labradoodle rump, and the sound alerted the zomb-pups.

The eight zomb-pups, mewling, *"Brains! Brains!"*, approached Cooper from all sides in the pitch dark. He couldn't see them, and the sound of his digging covered their cries.

Absorbed in the horror show in front of him, Shreddy nearly made a fatal mistake. *He forgot about Buster.* Then his whiskers tingled, and, in a heartbeat, every muscle in Shreddy's body contracted, launching him eight feet straight into the air. When he landed on the casing for the heat pump, Shreddy saw how near his escape had been.

Buster had been busy. His outraged baying of *"Braaaaaaains!"* was backed by an entire chorus of the chittering squirrels he had turned. *"B-b-br-ains! B-b-br-ains!"*

Shreddy shuddered and realized what a gigantic mistake he was making. Cooper might be the biggest waste of oxygen around, but the last thing Shreddy needed was more zombies.

Ricocheting off the wall of the house like only a crazy cat can, Shreddy leapt over the army of squirrels and shot into the night. His legs moved like he had eight of them.

At the edge of the garden, Shreddy surveyed his situation: squirrels and Buster behind him, puppies in front of him... and sizzling wires trailing into the awkward elm branch tangled into the rose bushes at the far side of the garden. *Is that what made them zombies? Or was it a weapon Shreddy could use against zombies?*

Electricity was powerful. Shreddy knew that from watching the red-haired woman use it to power the horrible monster she called *"Vack-ooom."* And Shreddy needed power on his side. So, creeping through flat iris leaves that marked the garden's edge, Shreddy approached the elm branch.

Lifting one paw at a time, placing each paw carefully, silently back on the ground... Shreddy moved unheard. But not unseen. He had failed to account for the mouse. She was no hunter, but she had proven easy prey for an undiscerning snake. And the snake's delectable brains had been in easy reach for the zomb-mouse from inside his esophagus. Together, they'd hunted down most of her kin. Zomb-mice littered the branches of the broken elm. Their beady eyes twinkled in the night. *"Brainszszss!"* their snake-maker hissed, and *"Brains!"* they all squeaked back in chorus.

With zombie armies on all sides, Shreddy froze in terror. At that exact moment, Cooper poked his nose up from the hole he'd been digging and woofed, "Found it!" Suddenly seeing the zomb-pups approaching him and the zombsnake trying to hypnotize Shreddy, Cooper became a dog of action. Grabbing the smartphone in his mouth like a tennis ball, Cooper charged straight into Shreddy, bowling the tabby cat right over. "Snap out of it!" he woofed around the phone in his mouth, a skill he'd practiced to perfection with tennis balls at the dog park.

Shocked out of his stupor, Shreddy tore away from the garden. Cooper was hot on his heels. The two of them ran as fast as they could down the block. Three houses... Four... Five, and they stopped.

"Zombies are sloo-ow!" Cooper crowed.

Shreddy glared at him. "They're at our *house*," he said. "We can't go home. And if we leave them there..."

Cooper looked stricken. "Susie! The red-haired woman!"

"Woah!" Shreddy yowled, stepping in front of Cooper. "What good will you do them if the zombies get you too?" *And*, Shreddy thought, *Cooper would be even more annoying as a zombie*. "We need a plan. We need tools."

"Well, we have the magic box," Cooper said, pawing it toward the angry tabby.

Shreddy grumbled at the smartphone. Its advice had failed him so far, but it was the compendium of everything he knew about zombies. Perhaps there was something he'd missed, something he could learn from looking at it. So, Shreddy stepped lightly on the icon for *Cars Vs. Zombies*, and the game maximized to fill the screen.

It had been running in the background, and as Shreddy squinted at the tiny icons, he realized something eerie.

In the game that was running, there were eight medium zombies arranged together; two crowds of smaller zombies, one of which was led by a large zombie and the other by a misshapen one; and one lone mega-zombie further away.

The eight medium zombies could be the zomb-pups; the

crowds were the squirrels led by Buster and the mice led by the snake. But then...

What was the lone mega-zombie?

Cooper barked just in time, and Shreddy pulled his straight-up aerial leap trick again. They both scattered away from the new zombie lumbering toward them. If Shreddy had thought Buster was bad, he hadn't counted on Dorothy —*the St. Bernard*—being resurrected.

"What's that?" Cooper barked as the two live-animals reconvened under Dorothy's front porch. The narrowness of the space there would protect them from her massive girth for now. But it would be no help against zomb-squirrels and zomb-mice when they got there.

"That's Dorothy," Shreddy meowed, his ears flat back and his eyes wide as a kitten's. "She died four years ago. Before that..." He remembered the one time Dorothy cornered him and got that slavering jaw of drool around his body and shook him. He couldn't talk about it. *"We need that smartphone."*

"The magic box?" Cooper asked.

"It's still on the driveway..." Shreddy said. His voice was a strangled whine, and Cooper proved himself forever brave (if not wise) in Shreddy's eyes by turning tail, shuffling out under the other side of the deck, and prancing around the yard, calling "Doro-zombie! Over here!"

Shreddy couldn't watch and squeezed his eyes as tight shut as they'd been when he was born. He realized he hadn't even been breathing when he felt the cool plastic of the smartphone nudged against his paws. In a gasp of relief, Shreddy opened his eyes to see Cooper looking at him. "Now what?"

The skittery figures on the screen were multiplying. Shreddy'd had no idea how many dogs had died in this neighborhood over the years. Nor had he figured on how many mice, squirrels, snakes, voles, chipmunks and other backyard vermin would fall to this deadly plague. And how quickly.

"Zombies sure are slow," Cooper barked again. "I could have made that big one chase me around all night!"

"Zombies might be slow," Shreddy said, ears flat and eyes wide. "But zombification is *exponential*. If this doesn't work..." He couldn't finish the thought. He couldn't even think it.

With a quivering paw, Shreddy touched the screen, setting off one of the iconic parked cars to zooming across the screen. With a cheerful electronic bleeple, the car skooshed the big zombie that represented Dorothy. *This had to work.*

Shreddy waited, fearing nothing would happen. But then the smartphone sent out its wireless signal invisibly through the air, and the snerffling, garrageling pile of putrid flesh and bone that had once been a St. Bernard lost its reanimation with a sudden *THUD!* A mere pile of re-death on the ground.

"You killed it!" Cooper said. "With the magic box! Do it *again!*"

Shreddy was quivering all over. He was terrified beyond words, but he touched his paw to another car icon. It took three tries this time, but Shreddy skooshed the snake zombie and a few mice.

For a moment, Shreddy and Cooper thought they were home free. Then they saw Buster, slavering zombie that he'd become, stumbling toward their hiding place. "Get him!" Cooper woofed. "Why aren't you killing him!"

"I'm trying!" Shreddy shrieked in a blood-curdling cater-waul. But, on-screen, Buster was protected from zooming car-icons by the army of squirrels and zomb-mice following him. Car-icons kept striking them down, but there were so many... And Shreddy's paws were shaking so badly, he couldn't kill them fast enough. Buster would be on them any moment.

Shreddy panicked and mashed the phone's power button, but turning it off had no effect. Buster and his army kept approaching. As Shreddy powered the phone back up, he cursed the precious moments he'd lost to this futile experiment. "Turn on! Turn on!" he yowled. "I have to play it... I need more *time*."

Gleaning the situation, Cooper earned his hero's stripes again. Darting out from under the deck, Cooper bayed to the moon like a lonely wolf. Glittering, rodential zombie eyes turned to him, and zomb-Buster answered his bay with another that said, "*BRAINS!*"

The two dogs, living and un-dead, took off down the street. Cooper out-distanced Buster easily, but Shreddy could see on the glowing screen under his paws that the swarms of tiny zombies were multiplying. Zomb-rodents would soon surround him. Both of them. Hopefully, Cooper's sacrifice would be enough to buy Shreddy the time he needed.

Clearing his mind and drawing a deep breath under his whiskers, Shreddy played as he had never played before. His paw-pads fluttered over the screen, setting off car-icons with a precision he'd never mastered on the complacency of a warm couch. Zomb-mice and squirrels that dared approach his hidden den dropped like flies.

When Susie's unfortunate pack of zomb-puppies appeared drooling at the edge of the porch, with only the slightest twinge of conscience, Shreddy re-killed them. When the path to the large zombie-icon representing Buster cleared, Shreddy struck him down with a combo-move involving two cars and a truck.

It was an exhilarating and proud moment for Shreddy when he finally looked out at the battlefield and saw he'd cleared the entire yard, driveway, and street in front of him. All the corpses littering the lawn and cement were lifeless. Purely, straight-forwardly dead. He was safe.

The glowing screen at Shreddy's paws had lit up in fireworks, and all the car-icons were happily dancing. He'd seen the red-haired woman beat *Cars Vs. Zombies* many times before, but Shreddy had never won himself. Until now. But, now, the sweetness was embittered by the knowledge that Shreddy's brilliant combo-move had taken down not one zombie but two.

Shreddy had seen the second zombie appear right as he struck the killing blow. Right next to Buster. Right where Cooper had been...

Shreddy had wanted Cooper gone. But not like this.

PAYING brief homage at the overturned gravestones by now empty graves, Shreddy made his way back to his home. He bathed Susie's freckled snout gently when he found her asleep on the red-haired woman's bed. Then he joined her and their master for a dream-filled night of sleep.

He dreamed of flowers and sunshine and being young again. When he woke, Shreddy felt very, very old, and he didn't know how he'd tell Susie when she awoke that her lover was gone. He'd sacrificed himself for her, the red-haired woman, and... Shreddy.

The red-haired woman got out of bed, tried to flick on

the lights, and, when they didn't work, drew the window curtains open instead.

"Oh my goodness," she said, seeing the broken elm and toppled telephone pole. Throwing on a robe and slippers, she rushed out of the bedroom, and a minute later, Shreddy could see her outside the window looking at her garden. The dug up graves. The littered corpses. Shreddy closed his eyes trying to shut out the memories evoked by his vicarious experience of the red-haired woman's horror.

He felt Susie's cold nose touch his whiskers. "Where's Cooper?" she asked.

Shreddy's ears flattened, and he wondered whether he could manage to never open his eyes again.

"What happened last night?" Susie said. *"Where's Cooper?"*

A cheerful voice that didn't sound like it belonged to a zombie barked, "I'm here!"

Shreddy's eyes shot open. "You died!" he spat. "I saw Buster... right before he died..." Shreddy eyed Cooper skeptically. *If you were dumb enough, could being turned into a zombie make you smarter?*

"Right before Buster died?" Cooper said. "There was a road kill raccoon in the street. If there hadn't been, Buster might have got me! But then he was busy eating raccoon brains... It was awfully close."

Cooper bounced onto the bed next to Shreddy and Susie. Any other day, Shreddy would have hissed and scratched the impudent yellow dog. This time, although his fur fluffed reflexively at having his space intruded upon, Shreddy stepped lightly away, ceding the bed to the dogs. He wasn't even too angry when the red-haired woman returned and gave both dogs hugs, grateful they were safely inside after the turmoil of last night's storm.

"I think," she said, "we won't be having any more puppies for a while." In her eyes, Shreddy could see the horror of the hordes of re-dead zombies littering her lawn, emanating outward from those turned up graves. He was glad some good would come of that. Even if he was stuck with Cooper.

The red-haired woman never did find her phone under the porch three houses down where Shreddy left it. When the replacement came, Shreddy was glad to see she didn't download the app for *Cars Vs. Zombies* again. Instead, she downloaded its sequel, and Shreddy had very mixed feelings every time he watched her play *Cars Vs. Ninjas*.

3

SHREDDY AND THE SILVER EGG

THERE IS nothing better than a patch of early evening sunlight, especially with the quiet strains of an opera playing on the Red-Haired Woman's television in the other room. There is nothing worse than watching an uncouth dog, lolling unappreciatively, in the single square of sun left on the kitchen floor, insensible to both the golden warmth and the soft singing in the distance.

Shreddy bristled the gray-striped fur along his back and flexed his claws. The day's sunlight would soon be gone, and Cooper was *wasting* it. Sure, Shreddy could have stalked over and swatted Cooper on the nose. The idiot blonde Labradoodle would relinquish the patch of sunlight easily enough, but then he'd be awake. And once Cooper was awake, he would bark. Shreddy wouldn't be able to hear the opera anyway. If he wanted sunlight, he'd have to hunt it elsewhere.

Shreddy decided to let the Labradoodle sleep in the sunlight that rightfully belonged to a cat by privilege of birth. Instead, Shreddy padded his way to the pet door, jumped through the flap, and planned to spend the tail end of the evening outside. At first, he thought to lie in the garden in his own backyard. Little purple flowers attracted the bumblebees, and it could be strangely pleasant to lie in the dirt, eyes slit shut, listening to the bumblebees buzz. He imagined their buzzing told tiny operas of its own.

Unfortunately, Shreddy found that the other dog who cursed his home—a freckle faced, curly eared spaniel named Susie—wasn't sleeping like her lover Cooper. She was bouncing around the yard, chasing the bumblebees. Shreddy always hoped she'd catch one, but she never did. He laughed inside at the image he pictured of her yipping and whining over the sting in her mouth that she would royally deserve. Ah well. A cat can't have everything.

As much as Shreddy enjoyed watching Susie make a canine fool out of herself, he wasn't in the mood for her antics. He wanted a restful evening, and he wouldn't find it in a yard graced by the prancing of a hyperactive Cavalier King Charles Spaniel.

Swishing his tail impatiently, Shreddy sprang onto the fence top and walked along the border of his yard. He considered sleeping under the red-leafed bush in the next yard over, but a kid in the basement of that house played drums. Badly. Besides, a crazy calico cat lived there, and he'd heard enough of her conspiracy theories to last a long while. So he continued on to the corner of the fence, leapt down into the alley, and trotted along the gravel alley road, keeping out an eye for a quiet looking tree with low enough branches.

None of the trees spoke to Shreddy that evening, so his trot around the block brought him right back to his own home, feeling twice as grumbly as before. Shreddy decided it was time to take his anger out on someone, and Susie was the obvious target. He hatched a plan to wait on the roof until Susie's yapping about the yard brought her in range, and then he would jump down—an angry feline bomber from above!

Yet, as Shreddy crouched, swishy-tailed against the edge of the roof, an even better target came to his attention: the sound of birdsong entered his flattened ears. High-pitched, twittery, and painfully shrill, the song danced from one octave to the next until Shreddy thought his ears would bleed. Simplistic and repetitive, it was the polar opposite of the Red-Haired Woman's beloved operas. Shreddy tried to ignore it, but his patience had already been worn thin, and the song sounded very nearby.

Abandoning his vigil at the edge of the roof, Shreddy crept paw-by-paw towards the peak of the roof and the source of the offending song. When he reached the peak, he peered over the top and looked down to see the new satellite dish that his owner, the Red-Haired Woman, had recently installed. Inside the curve of that electronic dish a gray and yellow bird, a Yellow-Throated Warbler, perched proudly on top of a small nest.

The Warbler's gray feathers blended into the plastic of the satellite dish, but the swoosh of brilliant yellow at its throat stood out as brightly as the sound of its voice.

A grumbly rumble of a growl broke out deep in Shreddy's chest, and the dancing birdsong came to a sudden halt. Shreddy cursed himself with a hiss. He'd never been a good hunter. And now, thanks to his angry growl, this bird knew exactly where he was hidden.

Tiny, piercing, black eyes stared at Shreddy. The Warbler's long, pointy beak—now tightly shut—tilted down towards its throat. Shreddy hadn't known a lot of birds, but he could tell this one was giving him a disapproving look.

"I'll peck your head if you come any closer," the little Warbler chirped.

Shreddy sniffed in laughter and lashed his tail in vicious merriment. "Then I'll claw your voice box out and eat it."

The Warbler tilted its head to the side and chirped, "If you could do that, you'd have done it by now."

Shreddy didn't like having a silly little songbird call his bluff. "All right," he hissed, "maybe I can't catch you. But this is my house, and I can make you miserable here. So, go build yourself a nest and make that horrible noise somewhere else."

The Warbler preened her yellow chest-feathers and fluffed her wings, pretending a casualness that Shreddy knew better than to believe was real. If he pounced on her, she'd be ready. She'd peck him on the head, and he'd look like a fool.

"I suppose you could do that," the Warbler said. "I didn't know this was a cat's house when I built my nest. There are two dogs that frequent the yard, and that usually means no cats. The dogs can't do anything to me but bark. Do you live with *dogs* then?"

Shreddy growled again. He didn't care for verbally sparring with this silver-tongued devil bird. "Never you mind about the dogs." He might not be able to get rid of Susie and Cooper, but he could certainly scare away this little stray bird. *She* didn't live under the Red-Haired Woman's protection.

To press his point, Shreddy crept over the peak of the roof, bringing himself almost a tail's length closer to the satellite dish and the Warbler's little nest. At that distance, he heard a ghostly echo of the Red-Haired Woman's opera in the electric buzz of the satellite dish. This was the perfect spot for his nap. He had to have it.

The Warbler tittered nervously and then whistled, "Look! I *would* move to another place and build a new nest, but I've already laid an egg here." The Warbler puffed up her chest proudly and shimmied back far enough on the nest for Shreddy to see the silver sheen of a large, oblong egg. "Who will take care of my little baby bird when it hatches?" the Warbler keened piteously.

Shreddy thought about that and realized he had a very simple answer. "I can do that," he said, changing his voice from the grumbly hiss he had been using to a lovely me-yowl. He straightened himself out, raising his ears and shoulders, until he sat in what he imagined to be a relaxed yet responsible looking pose.

"You?" the Warbler chirped skeptically, tilting her head to the side again.

"Yes," Shreddy affirmed. "I'd love to be a father."

"A *father?*" the Warbler chirped, incredulously. She twisted her head so far to the side, it almost turned upside down.

"Indeed," Shreddy intoned in a conversational meow. "House pets can't have children, unless their masters let them." Shreddy thought briefly of the dark, horrible days when the Red-Haired Woman used to breed Susie and Cooper for stupid, curly-haired puppies. Shreddy shuddered. "There could be nothing better than to have a tiny baby to care for." He hoped the Warbler couldn't hear the undercurrent of distaste in his voice. He tried to cover it by remembering that he, of course, would not care for the baby that hatched from this egg. No, he would eat it! And it would probably be very tasty. Young and *fresh.* Perfectly tender.

"Indeed," the Warbler chirped, echoing Shreddy's choice of words. She had raised several nests' worth of eggs before, and, although she always felt obligated to stay and care for the hatchlings to the best of her ability, she had to admit the appeal of being offered the chance to fly the coop. "Well..." she trilled.

"You can always come back and check on the little fledgling," Shreddy said, chuckling to himself on the inside about the pile of bones she'd find on the abandoned eggshell when she came.

Then Shreddy thought of the final detail that pushed him over from conniving cat to caring surrogate father in the Warbler's eyes: "In fact," he meowed, "you'll have to come back, because someone will need to teach the little fledgling how to fly."

The Warbler's tiny heart glowed warmly in her yellow feathered breast. She'd lost her mate recently and had been looking forward grimly to the necessity of having to face the duties of raising this particular fledgling alone. A daunting task, especially coupled with the troubled reservations she felt about this unusual, singular, clutch of eggs. So large. So silver.

The interest that the tabby cat before her showed in the well-being of her own un-hatched child won her over completely. "All right," she whistled. "You can raise the hatchling, but I'll be back when it reaches the age of fledgling."

Shreddy smiled with his eyes and refrained from licking his chops.

"You'll have to sit on the nest to keep the egg warm," the Warbler chirped, climbing off of the egg herself. She hopped out of the nest and perched on the edge of the satellite dish. "Then, once the egg hatches, of course, you'll have to fetch our baby insects to eat."

Shreddy nodded solemnly, slinking closer to the nest.

"The hatchling will prefer its insects pre-chewed," the Warbler admonished. "You can do that, right?"

"Of course!" Shreddy meowed. "Chewing on insects is a small price to pay for fatherhood."

"Well, that's true," the Warbler replied, thinking about how much more freedom she'd have to fetch insects for herself to eat now.

If the Warbler still had reservations in her motherly heart, they were waylaid—although not entirely laid to rest —by the sudden, startling surge of electricity that she felt in the air. Her feathers fluffed, and she felt horribly relieved that she'd be away from the smell of ozone and the slightly audible buzz soon. She promised herself that she'd never make a nest in one of these strange, electronic dishes again. They were simply too disconcerting. She only hoped that all these electric surges hadn't harmed her egg. She was almost certain they were why it had come out all shiny and silver.

The Warbler took to wing and flew away, hoping that the handsome tabby cat crawling into her abandoned nest behind her would take good care of her egg while she was gone.

Shreddy's first move in possession of his very own bird's nest was to take an extremely satisfying cat nap. The nest proved surprisingly comfortable, built more from stolen strands of hair and blades of grass than from any prickly twigs. Yes, Shreddy realized, he would enjoy keeping this tasty morsel warm until it hatched. It would be no problem escaping the drudgery of life with Cooper and Susie to take his daily catnaps in this cozy nest far removed from the stress of the ground-level world.

Shreddy purred and, for a moment, he imagined that he

felt a soft answering rumble from the silver egg, smoothly nestled against his fur. But it was only the buzz of electricity and the faint sound of opera in the air.

Days passed, and the buffoonish dogs began to notice Shreddy's disappearances. Cooper didn't seem to care; he was too busy searching the house for socks to eat. Susie, however, was curious, but her yapping inquiries were met only with the mysterious half-smile of a cat with a secret. A cat who soon hoped to have feathers in his mouth.

On the day that Shreddy finally felt the silver egg twitch beneath him, the sun was hot on his back. He was warm and content; it was almost an irritation to be interrupted by an ill-timed snack. Yet, Shreddy's belly growled and his mouth watered as he watched the cracks spread over the surface of the silver egg shell. Such a large egg would yield a satisfying meal, and Shreddy looked forward to crunching on the bones when all the meat was gone.

The sharp point of a black beak poked out, knocking a hole in the shell. Bright eyes stared through the hole at Shreddy. Then the hole grew, widening the cracks and splitting the egg down the middle. The creature inside stretched: a tangled mass of wet feathers, squirming to find its way out of the egg.

Shreddy narrowed his eyes. Something was wrong. In addition to talons and wings, this bird had paws. In place of tail feathers, it had a long, thin, twitching tail. The gray-striped feathers on its head and shoulders gave way to gray-striped fur. And the bright eyes—they were slitted emeralds that stared back at Shreddy like the Red-Haired Woman's mirrors.

Shreddy's fur fluffed out. He could feel his tail thicken into a brush. "What demon spawn are you?!" he spat. "Half-kitten, half-bird monstrosity!" His back arched, and he raised a paw to strike the hideous hybrid dead. There was no room for griffins in his world.

Then the pointed black beak opened, and a mewling call escaped the creature's throat. Its voice was more kitten than bird. That stayed Shreddy's paw and saved the creature's life.

Shreddy backed away from the nest, pressing his body low to the surface of the roof. He crept backwards to the bricks of the chimney, and hid behind its corner. Safely protected, Shreddy watched the baby griffin thrash and flail, finding its way out of the egg. It took a while for the griffin to figure out that its feet went down; the head went up; and the wings stretched and flapped uselessly. All the while, it kept crying, mewing for a mother.

Or father?

Shreddy flattened his ears, hoping to block the sound of the kitten's voice—the *bird's* voice. If he could see it as a bird, he could eat it.

If he could see it as a monster, he could abandon it.

It had the same vivid yellow swoosh of feathers under its throat as the Yellow-Throated Warbler who'd laid it, but it had Shreddy's stripes.

Shreddy yowled in anger, frustration, and distress. He didn't want this burden. He wanted a snack. But when his mouth filled with feathers, he didn't work his jaw with the vise-like grip of a mortal blow. He didn't crush the mewling baby's neck between his teeth. He lifted it gently by the feathered scruff of its neck and set out to find Susie.

The Cavalier King Charles Spaniel's floppy ears shifted slightly forward with interest when she saw the mewling creature in Shreddy's mouth. Her freckled nose twitched as she smelled it. Then she hopped backward, suddenly startled, as if she only now discovered the oddity of the writhing babe: her eyes may have seen it, but it took her nose to believe.

"It's a cat-bird!" she woofed.

"It's a *griffin*," Shreddy grumbled, spitting the feathery mass out on the ground of the garden. The Red-Haired Woman liked to read fantasy novels, and Shreddy would sometimes read over her shoulder. He knew about griffins and all sorts of things that dogs who couldn't be bothered with literacy knew nothing about. Somehow, none of his reading had prepared him for this.

He didn't know how to be a mother, and he didn't want to.

"I... uh... know how you've missed your puppies," Shreddy said to Susie, doing his best to sound sympathetic and ingratiating. It didn't suit him. "So, I found you this griffin to raise. It's like a really, really special puppy."

Susie tilted her head and narrowed her accepting, brown eyes. She could be so easy to trick at times. But not always. "That is not a puppy," she said, her voice cold.

"True..." Shreddy acknowledged, thinking quickly of ways to salvage the situation, "it's *better*." Instead, he made it worse.

Susie sniffed and turned away. "Then I'm sure our master can sell it for a good price," she woofed over her shoulder before scampering off.

Shreddy was left alone with a hungry baby half-breed. There was nothing for it but to start hunting for bugs. Shreddy didn't relish the idea. He loathed it. But, he couldn't find enough coldness, even in his curmudgeonly heart, to let the mewling thing starve. There was nothing for it but to begin hunting up bugs.

Shreddy dragged the mewling lump of fur and feathers

with him to an abandoned lot in the next block over to begin hunting. That way, he could keep an eye on the griffin, and he wouldn't have to explain himself to either Susie or Cooper.

Perhaps if Shreddy were more of a hunter, he'd have enjoyed the *prowl, wait, pounce* of catching flighted insects. But he wasn't. So, after batting uselessly at a few butterflies while the baby griffin watched and mewled, Shreddy realized he'd need a better strategy. The griffin's mewling had taken on a hopeless, despairing tone. Shreddy needed to catch some insects soon.

Shreddy found himself relegated to digging up pill bugs and centipedes from the dirt under rocks. Shreddy was hard pressed to think of a job more ill-suited to an intelligent, refined feline like himself. The dirt caked in his claws, and the dust raised by his digging made him sneeze. But at least the bugs were plentiful.

Unfortunately, the baby griffin turned out to be every bit as incompetent as that dratted Yellow-Throated Warbler said it would be. Instead of eating the big, juicy centipede right in front of it, the baby griffin just opened its beak and stared at Shreddy. Utterly useless. Shreddy tried cramming the centipede into that wide-open beak. For a moment, Shreddy thought that would work, then he realized the baby was choking.

Shreddy spent the afternoon grinding up centipedes and pill bugs in his teeth, a truly disgusting job, so that he could cram them into the baby griffin's seemingly bottomless gullet. When the griffin finally fell asleep, Shreddy's ears were flat from the humiliation of it all, and he could feel bug legs stuck between his teeth.

Not sure what else to do, Shreddy carried the baby griffin, gently by the nape of its neck, back up to the nest on the roof. Exhausted as well, Shreddy curled up beside the snoring baby half-breed. That small knot of warmth, a mere ball of fur and feathers, pressed against Shreddy's side. His breathing slowed to match the steady, slow breaths of the griffin's sleep. It was incredibly soothing. Almost enough to make Shreddy forget his hard day of digging up bugs.

The next few days were a blur of centipede chomping. More than a few times, Shreddy was tempted to trade the icky-crunchy bugs in his mouth for a taste of the tender morsel he was catching them for. Then the griffin would look at him and mew, sounding for all the world like a kitten, and Shreddy's resolve would fail him again.

Fortunately for Shreddy, Yellow-Throated Warbler chicks fledge quickly. While the half-breed did not grow as quickly as a warbler, it did grow faster than a kitten. Before the end of the week, the baby griffin could eat centipedes all by itself. A few days later, it picked up the skills necessary to catch them itself, as long as Shreddy pointed it toward an appropriately upturned rock.

As the griffin babe grew more independent, it also grew larger. Its feathered body grew too big for Shreddy to carry it up to the rooftop nest before its dexterity allowed it to climb up after him. Shreddy decided they should move to a pile of old, dirty towels that the Red-Haired Woman had thrown into a corner of her garage. That way, the mysterious creature could escape the Red-Haired Woman's notice.

Unfortunately, not everyone thought that the pile of dirty towels was beneath notice. After only one night nesting there, Shreddy found himself hounded by an irate Cooper.

"Hey Cat!" Cooper woofed when he found Shreddy in the backyard. He held his curly-haired head low in a battle-ready stance. "What were you doing in the garage last night? Your smell is all over my towels!"

Shreddy's fur fluffed along his back, and he carefully positioned himself to block Cooper's view of the little griffin, clawing at rocks with its talons behind him. "What?" Shreddy meowed. *"Your* towels?" *Why would Cooper care about a bunch of old towels? His scent wasn't on them, so he didn't sleep there.*

Cooper growled. Shreddy had rarely seen the buffoonish dog so menacing. Sure, he was an annoyance, but he was usually a good-natured one.

Most of Shreddy's methods for dealing with Cooper involved being in a high place that Cooper couldn't reach or hiding behind an object that Cooper didn't fit behind. From such positions of safety, Shreddy could shout insults and threats with impunity. He had time to work his verbal, intellectual magic on the gullible canine and convince him of half-truths, plausible untruths, and the occasional ridiculously, wildly, made-up story.

(Once Shreddy convinced Cooper that cats were immature humans, and human children were adult dogs—so, eventually, Shreddy would grow up to be just like the Red-Haired Woman while Cooper and Susie would grow into imbecilic toddlers. That one still made Shreddy chuckle. And, occasionally, he could still see Cooper look very confused by the interactions between dogs and children on the Red-Haired Woman's TV.)

Right now, though, Shreddy couldn't afford to escape up the nearest tree or into the tight space under the back porch. He had to protect the griffin. And that meant, he had to face Cooper on even ground.

Hissing and spitting, Shreddy puffed himself up and showed his claws. The baby griffin picked that moment to lose interest in the rocks and came peeking out around Shreddy's paws. "Who?" it chirruped, looking at Cooper and sounding for all the world like a baby owl. Shreddy could not have been more embarrassed.

"What's that!?" Cooper barked, his ears standing up as much as floppy ears can. He snuffled his nose closer to Shreddy's young charge than Shreddy felt comfortable with. Shreddy hissed again, but Cooper had clearly already tuned out his hissing and spitting.

Gathering all his restraint as his heart pounded for the baby griffin's safety, Shreddy changed tacks. "It's a very dangerous monster," Shreddy said.

Cooper's eyes widened and his nostrils flared in alarm. "I'm not afraid!" he woofed. "I'll kill it to protect you, Susie, and our master!"

"No!!!" Shreddy meowled, cowering away from Cooper while keeping his body over his tiny ward. "It's poisonous... to dogs! You have to leave it to me."

Cooper tilted his head, skeptically. "Poisonous to dogs but not to cats?"

"Yes," Shreddy said, feeling like he may have gained the upper paw again. "It's like the opposite of catnip." One of Shreddy's most embarrassing memories involved Cooper and Susie watching him get strung out on catnip and chase his own tail like a stupid puppy. So, Cooper knew about catnip. "In fact, it's a catnip monster. They're called catnip monsters, because they live in fields of catnip and eat catnip. The pungency of their diet counteracts and masks their usual poison, making them safe for cats. And only cats."

Cooper's curly eyebrows raised in surprise. "Woah, it's really lucky that our master has you here to save us then. You kill it."

"I was going to..." Shreddy said, looking down at the

harmless baby griffin between his paws and realizing that his own story had got away from him. "But I don't like to be watched."

Cooper shook his head. "If it's as dangerous as you say, then I need to make sure you've done the job right."

"Okay..." Shreddy looked up at the treetops, searching for a way to distract Cooper and give himself a chance to escape with the babe. His eyes settled on an old bird-house, hanging in the branches of an oak. A bird family had lived in it, years before, but now it buzzed with the coming and going of bees. "If you won't leave me to my task, then maybe you can be some help. See that bird house?" If watching Susie try to catch individual bees was amusing, then Cooper trying to catch an entire hive would be that much better. Though, he supposed he wouldn't have time to stay and watch.

Cooper turned his head, following Shreddy's gaze. His ears flopped as his head twisted and turned until he finally spotted the bird house. "Yes," he woofed.

"The safest way to destroy a catnip monster is to trap it inside a birdhouse. Bring me that birdhouse."

Cooper stared at the birdhouse for awhile, then he looked down at Shreddy incredulously. "You're not making any sense," he woofed. "And I'm never going to attack that beehive, no matter how many times you ask me to."

Shreddy had picked the wrong lie. He'd forgotten that he'd tried to trick Cooper into attacking the beehive before. Caring for this little creature was muddling his brain. Shreddy had spent weeks devoted to feeding, caring for, and protecting this baby griffin. He was turning into something he'd never wanted to be. A zombie. Or a parent. If there was a difference. Maybe it was time to move on?

"Well, what do you expect?" Shreddy snapped. "I've

been hanging out with a catnip monster. You've seen me on catnip."

Cooper moved forward and sniffed the baby griffin. "It doesn't smell anything like catnip. It smells like my pile of towels."

Shreddy sighed. "All right, you've caught me. It's not a catnip monster; it's a towel monster. I stole it from your pile of towels. It spontaneously generated there, and I didn't want you to know about it. I wanted to keep it for myself."

Cooper sniffed the griffin again and then looked very proud. "I knew those towels were valuable! That's why I was saving them." He shoved his muzzle against the little griffin and gave it a big sloppy, slurpy kiss with his tongue. The griffin purred.

Shreddy didn't know why he'd tried to protect the griffin from Cooper in the first place. The oaf was harmless. In fact, he'd probably make a tolerable baby-sitter, and Shreddy could clearly use a break. "Look," Shreddy meowed, "the little guy is hungry and looking for centipedes under rocks. Just follow it around and make sure it doesn't get hurt, okay?"

"Okay!" Cooper woofed. "Where are you going?"

"I'm going to go take a nap."

Freed of his parental responsibilities for the first time in nearly a month, Shreddy went into the house and curled up on the middle of the Red-Haired Woman's bed where he slept more soundly than a self-respecting cat should. This was no cat nap. This was the sleep of the dead or, at least, the dead tired. His ears didn't twist about, listening for threats to his small ward. His tail didn't twitch, keeping the rhythm of his annoyance. He didn't dream about the Yellow-Throated Warbler, returning to sing her horrible songs at him and finally take the griffin babe off of his paws. He merely slept.

Shreddy awoke feeling deeply rested. He felt much more his usual self—a cranky, individualistic, tabby cat who wanted nothing to do with a ridiculous half-bird mongrel. If Cooper wanted the little soul-crushing bundle of responsibility, then Cooper could keep it.

For the rest of the day, Shreddy skulked about, enjoying quiet patches of sunlight, watching dust motes dance, and relaxing the way that a cat of a certain age should. When night came and Cooper didn't join him and Susie on the Red-Haired Woman's bed, Shreddy wondered briefly how he and the griffin babe were faring. Mostly, he enjoyed the extra space.

Though, in the middle of the night, Shreddy missed the small bundle of feathers and fur cuddled at his side.

In the morning, purely for curiosity's sake, Shreddy decided to check on Cooper and the griffin. He looked for them in the garage, but they weren't sleeping on the pile of old towels. He looked all around the yard, but he couldn't find them. Finally, Shreddy heard a disturbing howl from the abandoned lot on the next block.

It sounded like Cooper's voice, so Shreddy took off running. He told himself that if something horrible was happening to Cooper, he wanted to see it.

Shreddy ran so fast that his four legs looked like eight. As he approached the abandoned lot, a second voice— warbling and soft—joined Cooper's howl. Shreddy slowed down. If the griffin was alive, there was no need to damage his dignity by letting Cooper see him hurry.

Among the patchy grass and bare dirt of the abandoned lot, three tree stumps stood, flat and short. Cooper and the griffin each sat on one of them, muzzle and beak turned to the sky as they howled at the pale day-face of the moon.

"Shreddy!" Cooper howled, seeing his companion cat.

In a sweet, trilling voice, the griffin echoed him, "Shreddy!"

In spite of himself, Shreddy's heart melted like butter to hear the griffin babe call his name. "What are you doing out here?" he meowed. "Why were you howling?"

Cooper shook his curly fur out of his eyes and woofed, "I was teaching Egypt how to sing."

"Egypt?"

"It's short for One Hundred Percent Egyptian Cotton," Cooper woofed. "Like the towels. Here, listen to us!"

Cooper began howling again. The tuneless wail filled Shreddy's ears, and his claws began to unsheathe. Then the griffin babe's voice joined in, tremulous but sweet. Shreddy recognized the song. It was the same song the Warbler mother had sung in her chirpy soprano. In her bird's voice, it had been the embodiment of a headache codified into soundwaves. In the deeper, rounder tones of the griffin babe, Shreddy could hear joy and springtime in the song. He could appreciate the beauty of how it danced upward from one octave to the next, finally ending in a soaring crescendo.

Cooper howled on for several bars after Egypt finished. Then he woofed, "Don't we sound fantastic?"

"Halfway," Shreddy allowed.

"We could use a few more voices. Do you think my towels will *spontaneously generate* any more towel monsters if I wait long enough?" Cooper looked like he was taxing his memory to the limit in recalling the phrase *spontaneously generate*.

Shreddy rolled his eyes. "Egypt's not a towel monster.

She's a griffin, and I hatched her from an egg that a bird gave me."

Cooper stared at Shreddy for a long time, then he turned and stared at the little tabby griffin. The gears in his brain, limited though they might be, were clearly turning. "That explains why Egypt looks like you. And a bird. If the bird comes back, do you think she would give me an egg? Or several?"

Suddenly, Shreddy knew what Cooper was picturing: half-Warbler, half-Labradoodle—an annoying, curly-furred puppy with wings and a high-pitched, tuneless voice. Or worse, an entire choir of them. Such a cacophony must never, ever be. It was Shreddy's worst nightmare.

"God no!" Shreddy yeowled. Then he remembered the buzz of electricity and the ghostly echo of opera in the satellite dish on the roof. Without that buzz, the Warbler would probably have laid a normal egg, and Shreddy would have hatched a snack rather than a responsibility.

Cooper couldn't get up on the roof, so Shreddy was safe from puppy-griffins. As long as he was safe, there was no need to lose a good motivating force for Cooper. "I mean," Shreddy said, turning his voice back to a solicitous meow, "you'd have to ask her. She'll come back when Egypt is ready to learn to fly."

"She will?" Cooper woofed.

"I bet, if I told her that you were really helpful and responsible with Egypt... Well..." Shreddy didn't have to finish baiting the hook. Cooper had already swallowed the whole fishing pole. He woofed and pranced about like an idiot for several minutes, and then he practically begged Shreddy to let him keep babysitting Egypt.

For the rest of the week, Cooper did the lion's share of mothering Egypt. He helped her hunt bugs, slept in the garage with her at night, and continued giving her daily "singing lessons." Shreddy was so relieved to have the burden of responsibility lifted that he barely noticed he was spending all his time skulking along, following Cooper and Egypt around. It was strangely satisfying to watch Egypt snatch a flying bug right out of the air, and her melodic caterwauling during the "singing lessons" was so pleasant, often echoing refrains from the Red-Haired Woman's operas that he'd listened to in the satellite dish while Egypt was still an egg. Shreddy hardly heard Cooper's moronic baying behind it.

And, at night, well, Shreddy liked knowing he had the freedom to go inside and sleep on the Red-Haired Woman's bed any time he wanted to, but, when it came down to it, that pile of old towels was terribly comfy. And he loved the feel of Egypt's small, striped body purring beside him.

Shreddy wouldn't have minded his life continuing that way forever.

Griffins grow up, and Yellow-Throated Warblers come home to teach them how to fly. The silhouette of a songbird cut across the midday sky, casting a tiny, flitting shadow over the shrubs of purple flowers where bees buzzed, dodging Susie's snapping muzzle and, less successfully, Egypt's arrow-sharp beak.

Shreddy saw the Warbler first, and he felt a cold shell harden around his heart. He turned his back on the tableau of griffin and spaniel snapping at bees, but his ears turned sideways in spite of himself. He listened as Cooper barked excitedly, "Oh my gosh! It's your mother-bird, Egypt! She looks just like you! Except less like a cat... And smaller. But otherwise just like you!"

Egypt trilled in her musical voice, "Mother?"

Shreddy closed his eyes, but it didn't stop him picturing

the reunion behind him. He heard the Warbler twitter to her daughter; Egypt trilled back, sounding more like a bird than she ever had before. Meanwhile, Cooper woofed a bunch of nonsense about buying eggs with a trade of some *very valuable* towels.

Suddenly, Shreddy felt a cold nose against his face. He opened his eyes and saw Susie staring at him, concern in her soft brown eyes. It made him want to slash her wet nose with sharp claws, but he couldn't rally the energy.

"It's hard when puppies leave," Susie said.

"No, it's not," Shreddy said. "I loved it whenever the Red-Haired Woman sold your stupid puppies."

Susie was used to Shreddy, so she didn't flinch at his meanness. She just stared at him with those sympathetic brown eyes.

Behind him, Shreddy heard singing, and he recognized the refrain from one of the Red-Haired Woman's favorite operas in Egypt's voice. The little griffin was teaching the song to her mother. The cold shell around Shreddy's heart crumpled a little. The bird and griffin sang together, their voices blending and contrasting, dancing in a musical whirl.

The song ended, and Shreddy heard flapping. Suddenly, both Cooper and the Warbler's voices raised in a cheer. Egypt was already learning how to fly. She was really going to leave.

The cold shell around Shreddy's heart melted completely. "How do you stand it?" Shreddy asked Susie. "Knowing you'll never see your puppies again?"

Susie looked down. There was a quaver in her voice. "I say goodbye."

Susie left. Shreddy watched her walk up to the house and hop through the pet flap in the back door. Behind him, he heard flapping, twittering, barking, and suddenly an angry buzzing. Shreddy turned around and saw his little half-kitten way up in the air, clinging with front-talons and clawful back-paws to the swinging birdhouse that had become a beehive. The bees buzzed wildly about, but Egypt merely snapped them up, so many tiny snacks in her narrow beak.

Perched on one of the nearby branches, the Yellow-Throated Warbler said, "I could never catch bees. I'm not fast enough."

"She didn't get it from me," Shreddy meowed. "If I were fast, I'd have caught you instead of promising to hatch your egg, and none of this would have happened." He never would have heard his favorite opera in Egypt's silver tongued voice, and he never would have had to say goodbye.

"She must have got it from me!" Cooper woofed. "I've been giving her racing lessons as well as singing lessons!" He demonstrated his speed by chasing his tail, twirling around in tight little circles.

Shreddy wasn't sure if he was tired from all the emotion involved in watching his little griffin grow up or whether his weeks of parenthood had mellowed him, but he didn't even bother mocking Cooper.

For the rest of the day, Shreddy watched Egypt learn how to fly. Her gray striped wings flapped clumsily at first, but soon she was soaring and singing as she soared. Snatches of opera floated down to him from the roof, the branches of the trees, everywhere that she disappeared to in the sky. Each time that Egypt chased her tiny songbird mother off into the distance, Shreddy wondered if that was the last time he'd see her. Then her melodic voice grew louder as she flew back again.

Shreddy never did follow Susie's advice. Not exactly. He watched the sky ripening into the gold and plum colors of sunset for a long time before he realized that he couldn't hear the opera anymore. Egypt wasn't coming back this time. He ignored Cooper barking at the beehive, asking the bees to join the choir he was starting. Finally, he went inside, found the last patch of sunlight for the day on the kitchen floor. He stretched out, felt the warm light on his fur, listened to the television playing opera in the other room, and, inside his heart, he said goodbye.

4

SHREDDY AND THE CHRISTMAS GHOST

EVERYTHING WAS GOING WRONG this Christmas, and the dogs were too stupid to care.

Usually, after the Feast of the Giant Bird, Shreddy and the dogs were given table scraps to eat. As a cat and a mediocre hunter, Shreddy relished the chance to taste the flesh of an avian larger than himself. He looked forward to it all year. Thus, he watched in utter horror as one of the Red-Haired Woman's dinner guests scraped all the plates off into the trash. No taste of turkey this year.

Despite this affront, the two dogs—Cooper the Labradoodle and Susie the Cavalier King Charles Spaniel— scuttled around the guests' feet, wagging their tails and collecting pats on the head as if nothing was wrong.

As if a pat on the head could make up for the loss of a toothsome bite of turkey.

Then it got worse. Instead of bringing home a fresh, fragrant pine tree—perhaps a luscious Douglas Fir or a savory Blue Spruce—the Red-Haired Woman brought home a cardboard box with a picture of a tree on it. When she opened the box, the inside reeked of plastic and was filled with a horrible mockery of tasty foliage. Metal branches and plastic needles. Nothing worth chewing on.

After she decorated the metal and plastic joke of a tree with the ornaments she kept in a shoebox, the Red-Haired Woman simply plugged the thing into the wall. The green horror lit up with tiny, colored lights, wired right into its branches. The lights twinkled like they were winking and laughing at Shreddy, while the Red-Haired Woman called out to Cooper and Susie, "Come on dogs! Time to go to bed!"

No! Seriously? This was not right!

The Red-Haired Woman was supposed to get out the Noisy Box That Makes Popcorn. Then she was supposed to sit and thread the fluffy kernels with red globes of cranberries onto chains for hours while Shreddy tangled himself in them. She was supposed to throw kernels of popcorn at the dogs who would jump to catch them. Shreddy didn't know why the dogs ate the things, since they tasted like packing peanuts, but Cooper always looked hilarious as he jumped around like a buffoon. Shreddy loved to watch Cooper look like a buffoon, and he loved to steal the fluffy kernels to bat them around the floor. Stealing from Susie was the best— she got these sad eyes and started whining. It always made Shreddy chuckle.

No chuckles tonight. Just glowering out the window.

The colorful little lights danced in the reflection on the window, but Shreddy stared past them into the darkness of the early December night. He could feel the cold of the night radiating through the window, and the chill made his back twitch, rippling the gray stripes of his fur. Shreddy was not a cat who enjoyed prowling through the cold, honing his hunting skills. However, when he noticed the sparkle of a tiny pair of eyes, staring up at him from a clump of frozen grass outside, Shreddy was struck with an idea.

A small, helpless mouse would be the perfect target to help him vent his anger. Mice need to die. It's good for them. And a good deed was exactly what an evening of such immense disappointments called for. It was the perfect way to get into the Christmas spirit. Shreddy hopped down from the window and ran for the pet door with his fat stomach wagging beneath him.

Shreddy almost rethought his plan when the frigid nighttime air hit his whiskers, but the memory of those hopeful, sparkling eyes steeled him. That hope needed to be dashed. Mice should not hope. How *dare* a mouse hope, when Shreddy was sad?

The mouse, weak from cold and hunger, merely stared at Shreddy and shivered. It didn't even run. Pathetic. Shreddy wasted no time on teasing or taunting the mouse. That would have kept him out in the cold longer.

The kill was quick and clean. Shreddy considered dragging the dead body back inside to leave under the abominable tree. But, so far this Christmas, the Red-Haired Woman didn't deserve a present.

Shreddy hurried back inside. Nevertheless, even in the warmth of the house, the cold stayed deep inside Shreddy's fur. He shivered himself to sleep.

SHREDDY'S DREAMS were haunted by sparkling mouse eyes. They hung on the Christmas tree, replacing the colored lights. They looked at Shreddy from Cooper's and Susie's faces. Then Shreddy saw himself reflected in the window, and beady mouse eyes looked back at him from his own feline visage. That startled Shreddy awake.

Grumpier than he had been the day before, Shreddy resolved to make himself feel better by torturing his canine housemates. He spent the day lounging behind the couch, occasionally meowing for Cooper to hear, entreating the dog to "Come play with me!"

Of course, Shreddy didn't want to play with Cooper, but the giant lump of a Labradoodle was too stupid to know that. He woofed and snuffled, shoving his curly-furred muzzle into the tight space between the couch and the wall, trying to fit, and whining, "I can't get to you!"

Shreddy almost felt happy when Cooper got his head stuck, but then the oaf of a Labradoodle got frustrated and started chewing on the couch. That's when the Red-Haired Woman put a stop to Shreddy's fun, deciding that the dogs needed a trip to the dog park.

Dog park, Shreddy grumbled. Talk about privilege. If Shreddy ran things, dog parks would be more like parking lots than playgrounds: owners would take their dogs there and *leave them*. Then the Red-Haired Woman would take Shreddy to a cat park, filled with slithering vines—fun to play with like snakes, but tasty like orchids—and dust motes dancing in the warm, sunny air.

Shreddy glared at the Christmas tree. It smelled unappetizing, but the twinkling lights *were* fun to watch. He let the lights' dancing patterns mesmerize him, hypnotize him, and call him closer. His weighty girth shook the tree as he placed his paws on the bottom branch. The metal spokes that comprised the cores of the branches bent as he climbed them.

Nestled comfortably near the top of the tree, Shreddy

found a little of the Christmas spirit for the first time that season. He idly clawed at some of the ornaments, feeling a surge of fondness for their familiarity. The ornaments were always the same: glass stars and icicles; crocheted snowflakes; and plastic figurines, including a dozen Santas in different poses; several reindeer; a mouse sleeping on a partially eaten sugar cookie; and a teddy bear angel on the top. There used to be little wicker creatures and origami polyhedrons, but Shreddy ate those years ago.

The memory of the wicker ornaments made Shreddy's mouth water. He felt like gnawing on something. Shreddy pondered the different ornaments surrounding him, but none of them were appetizing. That's why they'd lasted so many years.

Finally, Shreddy decided that, despite the wretched new plastic smell, the faux Christmas tree's bushy needles would have to do. Besides, it wouldn't really feel like Christmas to Shreddy if he didn't get a good mouthful of decorated tree.

As the bristly plastic needles filled Shreddy's mouth, he felt a kind of contentment. At least, their texture was good. Then he chomped down.

The moment Shreddy's teeth hit the twisting wires wrapped tightly around the branch's metal center, a shock bolted through his gums and all the twinkling lights went out. Back on. Out. And back on again.

Shreddy's fur fluffed out from ears to tail tip, and his heart pounded so fast he thought it would explode. His mouth tingled with the sting of electricity even after withdrawing his teeth, and he realized he was panting like a dumb dog. He couldn't help it.

At first, Shreddy was terrified. He wanted the Red-Haired Woman to come back and use her Magical Person

Powers to make him feel better. However, as the minutes passed, Shreddy was grateful that no one—especially Cooper or Susie—had been there to see his sorry state. And he was furious with the Christmas tree for tricking him into electrocuting himself.

Shreddy thought the ordeal was over.

Then he saw the ghost.

A translucent, rodential apparition with glittering, beady eyes hovered in the air, between the tree branches, in front of him. It was the mouse Shreddy had struck down the night before. The mouse whose eyes haunted his dreams.

Shreddy blinked, and the ghost was gone.

However, Shreddy soon noticed other disturbing changes to his senses.

THE CHRISTMAS ORNAMENTS WERE SINGING. The teddy bear angel was leading them in a rousing rendition of *Jingle Bells* —the Santas provided a solid chorus of altos; the three reindeer made for a catchy bass line; and the sleepy cookie mouse's voice rose above the others in a soaring, squeaky soprano. Almost anyone who heard them would have been quite charmed. But not Shreddy. He was horrified, and his ears flattened tight against his head, trying to shut out the cheerful music. It made next to no difference.

Either the shrill tones of happy Christmas singing pierced right through the thin layer of Shreddy's ears or else he was imagining the sounds and couldn't shut out his own hallucination.

Shreddy got out of the Christmas tree as fast as he could, which involved half climbing and half falling down through the brushy limbs. He spent the next several days skulking under the Red-Haired Woman's bed, as far from the Christmas tree as he could manage while staying in the warmth of the house.

Even there, all was not well.

The apparition of the mouse he'd slain continued to haunt Shreddy. Cold fingers tickled his back. Foul breezes like the breath of a mouse ruffled his whiskers and tormented his nose. He felt tugs on his tail, only to turn spitting and find no one there. And the soft squeak of a mouse's laughter woke him from his cat naps.

Harried and hassled, Shreddy sought refuge on the Red-Haired Woman's lap. Instead of her Magical Person Powers protecting him, though, Shreddy brought the Curse of the Dead Mouse on her. She twitched and squirmed, disturbed by the same rodential poltergeist, making her into a terrible, unsteady lap. Worse, her discomfort disturbed Susie, and the little spaniel took to woofing her head off, trying to impersonate a guard dog. Then Cooper picked up the hue and cry, and went barking about the house, not even knowing what had started it all.

Shreddy decided that was worse than the singing Christmas ornaments. Reluctantly, he returned to the mock-tree, hoping that the cheerful singing would keep the poltergeist away. Fight fire with fire. Fight hallucinations with other hallucinations.

FROM HIS PERCH in the middle of the tree, Shreddy watched the ornaments dance around the branches. The tree had been a frenzy of ornamental activity since Shreddy had climbed back into it. The twelve Santas had set up a betting pool, and the three reindeer raced for them, flying round and round the tree. Several of the Santas had sacks of toys from which to lay their stakes, but the other Santas took part by betting fur-lined boots and red hats. It was the strangest thing Shreddy had ever seen.

Shreddy watched with eyes dilated like a kitten high on catnip, wondering whether the Red-Haired Woman and the dogs could see the ornaments constantly rearranging themselves. Surely the Red-Haired Woman must notice that one of her Santa ornaments was wearing six hats while five others went hatless?

At the behest of the tree-topping angel, who felt that gambling was beneath a man as eminent as Santa—especially twelve men as eminent as Santa—the Santas moved on to rehearsing an all-Santa performance of the musical CATS. The reindeer made costumes for the Santas out of the crocheted snowflake ornaments while the Santas practiced their songs. Shreddy had to redefine his idea of the strangest thing he'd ever seen.

"Won't you guys ever go back to being inanimate plastic?" Shreddy asked the ornaments.

"Why would we want to be inanimate?" said the Santa wearing six hats. "This is much more fun."

Shreddy had a very different idea of fun than the Santas seemed to. However, even he had to admit that the ornaments' antics held a certain quality of fascination for him. Much more mesmerizing than they'd been before. And Shreddy had liked them before. That's why he hadn't batted them around and hidden them under the couch.

Shreddy, the three reindeer, the cookie mouse, and the teddy bear angel watched raptly as the Santas' rendition of CATS came together. No band of Santas could ever ask for a better audience.

When their final performance came to a close, the

cookie mouse crumbled the edge of her partially eaten sugar cookie and showered the performing Santas in a confetti of crumbs. The gesture was meant to be celebratory, though it proved in practice to be rather messy.

SHREDDY FELT HAPPIER and more peaceful than he had since the whole debacle of the faux-tree had begun. He settled into his perch, spread across the nexus of several branches, and closed his eyes for a good, long catnap, surrounded by the Christmas cheer of the ornaments.

Unfortunately, nearly as soon as Shreddy closed his eyes, the squeaking laughter of the mouse poltergeist began.

Stricken, Shreddy's eyes shot open. His ears flattened. And his heart began to race. He felt prickling little claws dance on his back, and his whiskers tingled. "No!" he meowled. "Go away, go away, go away!"

All the Christmas ornaments turned their eyes to him.

"What's wrong?" asked the cookie mouse.

"'Go away?'" growled the teddy bear angel. "This is our tree!"

"Not *you*," Shreddy breathed through his whiskers. "The *ghost*."

At the word *ghost*, the whole tree shook and shivered. The colored lights flashed on and off. And the temperature of the room dropped. Shreddy felt a powerful loneliness. A sense of isolation crept over him and consumed him. It was as if he'd never belonged to the Red-Haired Woman. As if he'd been a feral cat, wandering the streets alone and sleeping outside, his whole life.

He felt like a kitten again, small and shivering. The feeling took him deep inside himself—before the despair of being shut behind the bars in the animal shelter where the Red-Haired-Woman found him—all the way back to his first few weeks of life as a stray.

Shreddy felt a sensation of vertigo and nearly fell out of the tree. The feeling passed, but it left his fur twitching all over. He realized he was growling, high in his throat, and the pitch of his voice rose into a snarling hiss.

"What happened?" one of the hatless Santas asked.

All of the Christmas ornaments looked shaken, nearly as upset as Shreddy.

"It felt like there had never been Christmas..." the cookie mouse said.

The teddy bear angel said, "...and there never would be again."

The Christmas ornaments shuffled uncomfortably, hanging from their branches. Clearly, they'd all shared the same, disturbing sensation.

"Was that your ghost?" the Santa with six hats asked Shreddy. "Why is it haunting us?"

"It's haunting *me*," Shreddy meowed miserably.

"Why?" Six-Hatted Santa asked.

In a meow so small it was barely a mew, Shreddy said, "I killed it." His ears were still flattened, and he could still feel tingles in his whiskers.

The cookie mouse glared at Shreddy. "*Why* did you kill it?" she said.

Shreddy blinked. Such a strange question: obviously mice need killing. "I was trying to get into the Christmas spirit?" Shreddy said. That should be something a Christmas ornament would understand. Even a Christmas ornament shaped like a mouse.

The cookie mouse harrumphed at Shreddy. Clearly she felt more of a kinship with the mouse poltergeist—despite it being *real and evil* as opposed to *good and imaginary*—than Shreddy would expect. She pointedly turned her back to him, grumbling that he wouldn't get any more crumbs from her sugar cookie. Fortunately, Shreddy didn't have a lot of use for hallucinated crumbs of a plastic cookie.

"Look," Six-Hats said, "you're bringing ghosts around and upsetting our cookie mouse. I think you should go until you can sort out your issues. Christmas is supposed to be a happy time. And Christmas trees should be happy places. Not spooky, haunted, perches for Halloween cats."

Shreddy bristled. He was not a Halloween cat. "I'm a tabby! Don't you have eyes?" he hissed. "See the stripes?"

Of course, the raised fur along his spine and bushed out tail only helped prove Six-Hatted Santa's point. Shreddy did look like he belonged more in a haunted house than a manger scene. A Christmas tree haunted by living ornaments? That was more of a tough call.

Shreddy considered unleashing his wrath and unsheathing his claws on the ornaments. A Christmas rampage. But that would have taken energy, and all of his cat naps of late had been interrupted by ghostly squeaking. Instead, Shreddy slunk down through the faux-branches, planning to let out his suffering by yowling at the Red-Haired Woman until she felt as frazzled as he did.

As he reached the base of the tree, though, Shreddy heard the voice of one of the reindeer ornaments calling to him. With flattened ears, Shreddy looked back to see what the reindeer wanted. It was climbing down the tree after him.

When the reindeer arrived at the base of the tree, it said, "Don't take Santa's words too hard. It's a lot of pressure for him."

Shreddy skewed an ear forward to show he was listening but left the other one back in skepticism. "Pressure?"

The reindeer babbled something about competitive edges, generosity, and the soul-crushing quandary of losing one's uniqueness. Shreddy probably wouldn't have cared even if the reindeer weren't an hallucination. However, then the reindeer said, "Go find out what your ghost wants. Once you've laid that to rest, I'm sure we'll be happy to have you back here."

SHREDDY BLINKED. And the reindeer was gone. For a moment, he thought his hallucinations were over, then he heard the sounds of the Broadway musical "Camelot" from the branches above. The reindeer ornament must have simply scampered back up to his fellows. Still, it was an interesting idea the reindeer presented: what did the ghost want?

Shreddy had assumed the ghost wanted merely to torture him. But, if the ghost wanted something else, like a piece of cheese—*mice like cheese, so dead mice probably do too, right?*—then maybe Shreddy could fix this situation. And the mouse would go away.

This presented Shreddy with a new problem. He needed a piece of cheese, and the Red-Haired Woman kept the cheese in the Giant Sealed White Box of Coldness. There was no way into that box. Shreddy had tried to claw his way into it before.

However, Cooper did have a plastic, squeaky toy cheese. Poltergeists can't eat anyway, right? So, what difference would it make to the mouse poltergeist if the cheese was real or not?

Shreddy spent the rest of the day peering from around corners at Cooper. The empty headed Labradoodle was snuffling around the edges of rooms, occasionally licking the walls. He seemed occupied with his strange pastime. But Shreddy knew from past experience that Cooper had an uncanny ability to sense when a feline was stealthily approaching his dog bed filled with smelly rawhide and ridiculous squeaky toys. So, Shreddy waited patiently until Cooper flopped onto his side and passed out on the middle of the floor. He fell into a snory dog nap with his paws waving fitfully in the air. Shreddy made his move on the cheese.

Shreddy had to suffer the indignity of a withering look from Susie for stealing the toy, but she didn't bother to defend it. Squeaky toys sounded too much like they were shrieking in pain to her when she chewed on them, and she wouldn't risk hurting the innocent cheese herself just to rescue it from Shreddy.

Alone with the cheese, Shreddy tried several magical incantations to summon the rodential poltergeist to him. Of course, he didn't really know any magical incantations, so he mostly muttered under his whiskers, threatening the dead mouse with further deaths for itself and its living relatives (not that he really wanted to go to the trouble of hunting more mice) if it didn't reveal itself, accept the offering of cheese, and get out of his life.

The mouse poltergeist did not heed Shreddy's words. It did not appear before him. In a moment of lucidity, Shreddy pictured himself muttering over a squeaky cheese, at the advice of a reindeer ornament, and thought perhaps he'd lost his mind. He'd imagined it all. There were no singing Christmas ornaments. And there was no mouse poltergeist.

Then the maniacal squeaking began, and a wind that

smelled of rot and rain blasted his whiskers, causing Shreddy to flatten his ears.

"I don't want cheese!" The words squealed like claws scrabbling over steaming ice.

Shreddy meowed, his voice deep and hollow with the shock of a dead mouse talking to him, "What do you want?"

More than words, Shreddy felt a summoning inside himself: *Come to the place you struck me; come to the place you killed me with your paw.*

Shreddy wasn't a fan of the winter air at the best of times. At night, under the summons of a hostile ghost? It was all Shreddy could do to slink, fat stomach dragging on the ground, and tail tucked between his legs like a dog, out the pet door and into the yard. He left the squeaky cheese behind.

THERE WAS fresh snow on the ground outside. It went *crunch* and then *slick* under Shreddy's paw pads. Flakes in the air caught in his whiskers and made him sneeze. When Shreddy made it to the ground outside the window where he'd struck down the mouse, he breathed through his whiskers, "What do you want from me?"

Shreddy expected winds and squeaking as loud as thunder. Instead, a small ghostly figure appeared quietly on the snow in front of him. It was the mouse he'd killed, still shivering, but transparent. Shreddy's ears perked up, and he tilted his head. The poltergeist wasn't so frightening here. On an impulse, Shreddy reached out a clawful paw and swatted the vision, but his paw passed right through the mouse and struck the ground beneath.

"Eek!" the ghost mouse squeaked, jumping rather tardily from the spot. "You would kill me again?!!"

"Well," Shreddy meowed, "I had to try. Look, I don't like being haunted." He tried speaking reasonably to the mouse. "What can I do to make you stop?"

The mouse shivered and shuffled uncomfortably. "I don't know," it squeaked. "I'm not very experienced at this ghost thing."

Fighting the temptation to swat at the mouse again, Shreddy said, "A plastic reindeer I know suggested that you might want something, and that I needed to help you lay it to rest. Something like that. So, what do you want?"

The mouse scratched one of its ears with a tiny back paw. It looked like it was considering the question. Eventually, it squeaked, "What I really want is your life."

"Out of the question," Shreddy snarled. "What good would having you stop haunting me do if I'm not alive to enjoy it? Besides, a cat death for a mouse death is hardly a fair trade, because a cat's life and mouse's life are not of equal value."

The mouse surprised Shreddy by agreeing: "Of course they're not. You live inside a warm house with never-ending bowls of food and a person who loves you. I shivered and starved in the cold until you were cruel and kind enough to strike me down."

"Well, that's true," Shreddy said. Although, he couldn't help thinking that if the Red-Haired Woman *really loved him*, she would have given him a plate of turkey and a *real* Christmas tree to chew on instead of causing all this trouble.

Maybe if the mouse could just see how disappointing Shreddy's life truly was, it would let go and move on.

"I have an idea, mouse," Shreddy meowed. "What if I let

you live as me for one day. Can you do that? Take possession of me?"

"I can try," the mouse squeaked. The mouse's ghostly eyes narrowed, and its whiskers quivered in great concentration.

Shreddy felt a tingling in his whiskers and ear tips, but the ghost didn't seem to be strong enough to possess Shreddy without a little cooperation.

Shreddy pitied the ghost. He closed his cat's eyes, relaxed the tension in his ears and tail, and opened his mind. When Shreddy opened his eyes again, both Shreddy and the mouse looked out through them.

THE MOUSE's name was Whisperquick, and she'd lived in the yard of the Red-Haired Woman's house for the entire year and a half of her short life. Through their melded selves, Shreddy remembered the experience of mouse teeth nibbling on soggy popcorn and cranberry chains. The chains had dangled off the discarded Christmas tree last January, as it lay skewed and needleless on the edge of the street. For Whisperquick, it had been a glorious New Year's feast. For Shreddy, it had been a relic, thrown away with the trash.

Shreddy felt Whisperquick wondering whether there would have been more popcorn chains to look forward to if she'd lived, and his ill-tempered emotions instantly answered her question. Their minds were too close for true conversation.

Whisperquick's thoughts felt small and weak compared to Shreddy's, and he was confident he could push her out from his mind and body if he needed to. But, he was committed to seeing this to the end. He would show this mouse how little she was missing, and then she'd give up the ghost and be done haunting him for good.

With Shreddy's guidance to remember the way, Whisperquick walked her new feline body back to the pet door and inside of the house. It was nearly midnight. And, Shreddy realized when he saw the kitchen table with cookies and milk set out for Santa, that tonight was Christmas Eve. Whisperquick thrilled with excitement when she realized her one day as a pet would, in fact, be Christmas Day. Shreddy couldn't help sharing her excitement—her mind was too close to his for him to avoid it.

Despite Whisperquick's eager anticipation, she was saddled with a feline body in need of sleep. So Shreddy guided her to the Red-Haired Woman's bed where they curled up on the warm, cozy blankets next to the bump of her feet.

Neither cats nor mice dream of sugarplums. But Whisperquick's dreams, sifting through all the happy memories in Shreddy's head, were sweet.

They awoke the next morning in an addled daze—Shreddy wasn't used to his memories focusing so thoroughly on the *good* in his life, and Whisperquick wasn't used to waking up somewhere *warm*. The Red-Haired Woman petted Shreddy, scritching behind his ears and cooing "Good morning" and "Happy Christmas" sounds at him and the dogs.

Whisperquick was so startled by a human hand reaching for her that if she weren't already a ghost, she would very likely have died from fright. But, soon, she was purring and enjoying the caresses as if she'd been a cat and a house pet all her life.

❧

THE TRADITIONAL CHRISTMAS breakfast of scrambled eggs for the pets confused Whisperquick at first. To her mouse's sensibilities, the dogs' bowls on the floor—with smears of peanut butter on the eggs—smelled more appealing. But Shreddy's bowl of eggs was served on the counter with cream poured over it. Fortunately, the cat's body that Whisperquick inhabited was made for loving eggs and cream.

Next came the presents. The Red-Haired Woman always had new toys for them all. Cooper got a strange star-like object made from the same material as tennis balls. It bounced in wacky ways when the Red-Haired Woman threw it for him. Susie got a bright red plastic cube with balls hidden inside. It was a puzzle, and Susie immediately took to knocking it around the floor with her muzzle, trying to dislodge the balls.

Shreddy's present was a new Koosh ball that dangled from a stick. Cooper had eaten the last one, and Shreddy missed it sorely. He suspected this one wouldn't last long either. Although, it was hard to feel cynical while Whisperquick stared out through his eyes in amazement at every pedestrian detail of his life.

When the furnace roared to life, heating the room, Shreddy's feline body automatically stretched luxuriously in reaction. Shreddy took the warmth for granted; Whisperquick thought it was yet another generous Christmas gift from the Red-Haired Woman.

When the Red-Haired Woman invited Shreddy and the dogs to snuggle with her while she watched *Miracle on 34th Street*, Shreddy wanted to turn his nose up at her. He didn't like sharing her lap with clumsy, crowding dogs. Whisperquick, however, eagerly jumped into her lap. Worse,

Whisperquick cuddled up against Susie and gently bumped noses with Cooper. Shreddy almost cast the pathetic mouse ghost out of his body right then and there.

But he didn't want her to haunt him again.

And, strangely, the dogs weren't so bad to share a couch with once they settled down into watching the movie.

NOTHING REMARKABLE HAPPENED that Christmas evening. And, yet, everything was remarkable to Whisperquick. Every scritch from the Red-Haired Woman. Every soft cushion to sleep on. Every bite of food from Shreddy's normal, boring old bowl of dry cat food.

By midnight, Shreddy was exhausted from the constant feeling of joy and gratitude that Whisperquick radiated throughout his whole body, from paw pads to the tips of his ears and twitching tail.

Perhaps Whisperquick was exhausted too. For she gave up Shreddy's body without so much as a squeak of resistance. He didn't even have to ask. One moment, she was purring on the couch, watching the Christmas ornaments dance in the fake tree. The next moment, Shreddy felt a hollowness in the pit of his chest, and he saw the translucent shape of Whisperquick's mouse body crouched in front of him.

"You're ready to go now?" Shreddy asked, his voice still thick with all the purring Whisperquick had been doing.

Whisperquick's ghostly paws ruffled her whiskers. Then she said, "I don't know, but my time was up." She twitched her nose. Mice are so fidgety. "I've had my day. It was wonderful. Thank you."

"Er, yes, well," Shreddy equivocated. He didn't believe in

expressing gratitude, and he didn't know how to gracefully handle someone expressing it to him. "You're going to go away now?" he meowed hopefully.

"I guess that's only fair," Whisperquick squeaked. She sounded lost. "I..." She grabbed her tail with her tiny paws and threaded it nervously into loops and corkscrews. "I don't really know *where* to go."

Shreddy narrowed his eyes, and a rumble started deep in his throat. *After sacrificing his Christmas to this mouse, she still wasn't going to leave him alone?* Then he was struck with an idea. *Where better for an hallucination to live than with all the other hallucinations?* Shreddy grumbled to himself, "I have to do all the work." Then he unfolded his paws to get up from this warm spot on the couch. "Follow me."

SHREDDY LED Whisperquick over to the Christmas tree. The ornaments were arguing about whose turn it was to be the tree-topper, but an observant Santa noticed that Shreddy had returned. "Oh look, the Halloween cat is back," the observant Santa called out. Then, in the distraction that followed, the observant Santa scrambled for the top of the tree, successfully shouldering aside two other Santas and the reindeer who had previously been closest to the top.

The teddy bear angel glared up at the Santa, tut-tutting about the use of questionable tactics. The Cookie Mouse glared at Shreddy, as if no time had passed since Shreddy's confession of mousicide. All in all, it was a lot of glaring going on for the insides of a Christmas tree.

However, one of the reindeer lounging on a branch near the bottom of the tree welcomed Shreddy back, saying, "Have you cleared up that problem of yours yet?"

"Almost," Shreddy meowed. "My ghost and I have made peace with each other, but she doesn't know where to go now that she's done haunting me." Shreddy watched the Cookie Mouse carefully as he spoke his next words. "I thought I'd bring her here and introduce her around."

The Cookie Mouse didn't stop glaring, but her large round ears twitched with interest.

Shreddy looked around for his ghostly follower, but he couldn't see her anywhere in the faux tree branches. He hissed under his breath, *"Where did you go, Whisperquick?"* Then the branches started shaking, the colored lights flashed, and the maniacal squeaking of the rodential poltergeist began again. Shreddy's ears flattened, and he yeowled in fear, anger, and fury, *"Whisperquick!!!* I thought we were done with that!"

The shaking, flashing, and squeaking-laughter stopped. A bashful but translucent mouse appeared, perched on the tip of one of the branches. "Sorry," she said. "I was nervous."

The Cookie Mouse laughed. Her squeaking laughter sounded like tinkling Christmas bells, unlike the cacophonous screeching of the poltergeist laughter. "That was fantastic," the Cookie Mouse said. "You really know how to keep that cat on his toes!"

Whisperquick's translucent body blurred almost out of sight. Then it sharpened into a clearer form than Shreddy had seen her hold yet. "Thanks," she squeaked. "I like your sugar cookie."

"Want a crumb?" the Cookie Mouse asked, breaking off a piece of plastic that looked golden-buttery and delicious. Shreddy wasn't sure how the cookie was able to keep providing crumbs without seeming to diminish in size. Perhaps one shouldn't think too hard about the logic of hallucinations.

"I'd love a crumb..." Whisperquick said, regretfully. "I've never tasted sugar cookie, but..."

Whisperquick trailed off, and Shreddy finished her thought—he was in the practice of sharing thoughts with her: "You need a body to eat. Even a plastic body. Perhaps, you could give her yours?" Shreddy suggested helpfully. "You're both mice."

The Cookie Mouse wrinkled her nose at him. "Are you trying to kill me too?"

Shreddy had to admit to himself that the thought had crossed his mind. He chose not to admit it to the Cookie Mouse though.

"I think," said the Santa at the top of the tree, "that we can do a little better than that..." He began climbing down from the top of the tree, and, when he got down to the level of Whisperquick and the Cookie Mouse, he un-slung the brown sack hanging over his back. He opened the sack and with much bravado pulled forth a plush mouse doll. Well, a plastic-ornament model of a plush mouse doll. Shreddy was getting confused by the rules of this hallucination, but the Cookie Mouse and Whisperquick squeaked with joy.

"Perfect!" the Cookie Mouse said.

Whisperquick didn't say anything, but her ghostly presence lost its mouse-shape, becoming an amorphous, shimmery cloud that descended into the mouse doll.

The mouse doll, newly animated by Whisperquick, opened her previously inanimate eyes. After a few moments to orient herself, Whisperquick scurried out of Santa's hands and over to join the Cookie Mouse on her sugar cookie.

The two mice danced. The Santas applauded. And the reindeer sang a spontaneous round of "Joy to the World" in three-part harmony. Afterward, the teddy bear angel officially welcomed Whisperquick to their fold with a moving speech.

Whisperquick bowed her head in thanks, but she was too busy eating sugar cookie to say anything.

SHREDDY SPENT the next week watching the antics on the Christmas tree from a safe distance. Namely, the couch. He was hoping that the effect of his shock would wear off, and eventually the ornaments would go back to being inanimate. So far no luck. In fact, he was beginning to wonder if it would ever happen. He even wondered if the shock hadn't so much caused a massive, complex hallucination as it had simply dropped the scales from his eyes. Had the Christmas ornaments always been alive like this? Only, until his shock, Shreddy hadn't been able to see...?

After a week of pulling the balls out of her new puzzle toy and putting them back in, Susie tired of playing with her Christmas present. She took to sitting on the couch next to Shreddy, asking him what he was looking at. After a day of making up answers for her—"Dust motes," "Nothing, leave me alone," or "The ghosts of your dead puppies" —Shreddy tired of trying to make Susie go away and found it easier to just tell her the truth. "The Christmas ornaments are playing tag. Right now the Cookie Mouse is 'it.'"

Susie chuckled. "You're so clever," she woofed. "Cooper, come over here! Shreddy's making up stories about the Christmas ornaments."

Shreddy was torn between annoyance and feeling flattered. In the end, his ego won, and Shreddy gave a blow by blow account of the Christmas ornaments' games to his rapt audience of two dogs. He had to admit, he rather liked having them hang on his every word.

On New Year's Eve, when the Red-Haired Woman brought out the special shoebox to pack away the Christmas ornaments, Cooper and Susie howled pitifully to see them go. They wanted more stories!

Shreddy, however, was relieved. He was ready to be done with the holidays and get back to normal life. Though, he kind of hoped that when next year came, the Christmas ornaments would still be alive.

5

SHREDDY AND THE DANCING DRAGON

THE CARDBOARD BOX, labeled *Yay! PlayCube!* on its sides, was more than big enough to hold Cooper, the blonde, curly-furred Labradoodle. Yet, somehow, Shreddy knew better than to hope that the Red-Haired Woman had brought in such a large, sinister box for any reason as comforting as to haul the annoying Labradoodle away.

All three of the Red-Haired Woman's pets—Shreddy the tabby, Cooper the Labradoodle, and Susie the Cavalier King Charles Spaniel—watched as she sliced through the tape on the edges of the box and unfolded the top flap to open it.

The Red-Haired Woman drew out a strange bundle of white plastic cords and a big cube. The two dogs wagged their tails happily, excited to see what their brilliant master had brought home to make their lives more magical. Shreddy twitched his tail too, but, in the language of his feline body, that twitch meant anxiety. Unlike the dogs, he didn't think the Red-Haired Woman was a brilliant sorceress who conjured strange sounds from her smartphone and warm food from the kitchen out of nothing.

Shreddy loved the Red-Haired Woman, but he knew

about technology. It could be wonderful. It could also be dangerous. Either way, the Red-Haired Woman seemed to have different ideas from him about how to use it. He'd warred with her over technology before.

So it was with trepidation in his whiskers and schemes in his heart that Shreddy watched the Red-Haired Woman set up the white plastic cube beside the TV and hook it up with twisting, twining white cords. By the time she was done, the cords clung to the base of her TV like an octopus trying to strangle a diver.

Shreddy had seen ViewTube videos on the Red-Haired Woman's smartphone of octopi and their tentacle-happy ways. Nothing good could come from a piece of electronics that looked so much like one of those creepy monsters of the deep.

Shreddy lashed his tail angrily against the carpet as he watched the Red-Haired Woman take the knobby end of one of the weird white tentacle-cords in her hand. She pressed a button on the PlayCube, and the TV screen sprang to life with a flourish of music and flashy colors unlike any of the safe, wholesome videos that it usually played. The Red-Haired Woman withdrew across the room to her couch, where the two dumb dogs eagerly jumped up, mauling her as they settled onto the cushions on either side of her.

For the rest of the evening, Shreddy watched in horror as his Red-Haired Woman stared slack-jawed and zombiefied at the TV screen. She clutched the tentacle-cord's knob in one-hand, and she idly stroked Susie, curled against her side, with the other. All the while, techno-beats and synth-pop chords screeched from the TV speakers, assailing Shreddy's sensitive, feline ears, and an animated dragon danced on the TV screen.

Night after night, the demonic PlayCube with its

animated dragon summoned Shreddy's Red-Haired Woman to it. Hour after hour, Shreddy watched her life being sucked away. After a full week of the intolerable situation, Shreddy had seen more than enough. The PlayCube was more than a video game system—it was a portal into a parallel dimension. An *evil* dimension. It had to go. And Shreddy felt that Cooper should be the one to do it.

Until the PlayCube, Cooper was the worst thing the Red-Haired Woman had ever brought home. If Cooper had been a brighter dog, Shreddy might have considered him his arch-nemesis. As it was, Shreddy had to settle for considering Cooper a bumbling idiot and reserving arch-nemesis status for the crazy Calico who lived across the way.

Shreddy made his pitch to the curly-blonde Labradoodle to no avail. Cooper remembered the time that Shreddy had convinced him to bury the Red-Haired Woman's smartphone in the garden. That had not gone well.

"You're just angry," Cooper said, "because you don't know how to turn it on." He knew that Shreddy liked to play the games on the Red-Haired Woman's computer, whenever she left it running.

"The PlayCube is different," Shreddy spat through his whiskers. "It's *evil*."

"I like it," Susie commented, flouncing into the room with her curly ears flopping. She turned up her speckled nose at Shreddy and said, "When the master plays it, she lets me sit on the couch and snuggle with her."

Incited into immediate action by Susie's infuriating demeanor, Shreddy lowered himself to the carpet, raised his haunches and began to wiggle them in preparation for a terribly dangerous front-on pounce at the offending elec-tronics. Before he could launch himself at the PlayCube, however, he was bowled over and thoroughly woofed at by Susie.

"I told you! I like it!" she barked.

Utterly surprised by the force of Susie's conviction, Shreddy escaped to the top shelf of the corner bookcase and began licking his paw diffidently.

Never mind. He could wait. Susie couldn't defend the PlayCube all the time.

THE RED-HAIRED-WOMAN TOOK the dogs to the dog park the next day.

Shreddy knew better than to attack the PlayCube directly with his teeth—he'd learned the hard way not to chew on electric cords. But he'd seen the Red-Haired-Woman drop her smartphone in a banana-honey sandwich she was making once. The smartphone had been covered in sticky, gold honey, and she freaked out over whether it was destroyed. (It wasn't, but the Red-Haired-Woman didn't make sandwiches one-handed while playing games on her smartphone anymore.)

Shreddy could only assume that honey had magical powers to disable electronic devices. He could well believe it. The bees that lived in the garden were mysterious, mesmerizing creatures. Their buzzing held music and danger. A golden elixir drawn from a hive such as theirs must be powerful stuff.

If Shreddy could coat the PlayCube in honey, it would be safe to chew the dread thing to death.

The Red-Haired Woman kept the honey in a cupboard over the kitchen sink. Shreddy had learned how to open that cupboard long ago when she'd made the mistake of storing catnip there. Now she stored catnip in the refrigerator.

Shreddy perched on the edge of the sink, reached up to open the cupboard, and then jumped inside. He found the honey bear and clasped it with his jaw, teeth piercing its plastic belly. He shuddered at the shock of sweetness that oozed onto his tongue.

The honey bear was awkward and heavy for his jaw, but Shreddy held it tight in his mouth as he jumped down from the cupboard, trotted through the kitchen, and returned to the electronically haunted living room. He placed the honey bear on top of the PlayCube, and then he truly ripped into it, gnawing and clawing until it was a shredded, tattered, sticky wreck.

Honey dripped down the sides of the PlayCube.

Shreddy gave the honey a moment to work its magic. Then he set into the cords with a vengeance, gnawing down hard with his back teeth. His tail lashed. His eyes dilated with the satisfying joy of feeling his teeth sink right through the plastic coating of the cords and into the thin metal wires inside.

He didn't notice that he'd set his back foot on the power button until he felt the unmistakable ZAP of electricity in his mouth.

Shreddy jumped back, his paws tangled in the cords, and clonked his head on the hard plastic of the knobby controller.

A buzzing in his ears joined the tingling that lingered in his mouth. Shreddy opened his eyes; he didn't remember shutting them.

Although it was midday, the living room and the windows that looked outside had gone dark as night. Shreddy could still see with his cat's eyes, but he knew that something was very, very wrong. He looked up, and where the rectangular TV screen had been, there was a swirling vortex—black and purple, roiling like storm clouds, sparking with electricity. Nothing could have impelled Shreddy to enter that vortex, not willingly.

He wouldn't have done it to save the Red-Haired Woman's soul. He wouldn't have done it to save his own skin.

Yet, the twining white cords tightened around Shreddy. He struggled, but like an octopus dragging a diver into the deep, the white cords dragged Shreddy, spitting and hissing, into the vortex.

Wind battered Shreddy as he entered the swirling clouds. His ears popped, and his fur stood on end—not from fear but from static electricity. Then the wind died, and the air stood still.

The white cords dropped Shreddy on hard dirt, untwined from him, and withdrew back through the vortex that was now behind him.

Shreddy looked around the dark chamber that he found himself in. From this side, he could see his empty living room through the purple-swirling vortex. Other vortexes looked out on other rooms that he recognized from looking through the windows of other houses in the neighborhood —other houses with PlayCubes.

Shreddy considered jumping back through the vortex to the relative safety of his own living room, but his curiosity got the better of him. If the portal had carried him into a parallel dimension, how could he not explore it?

Cautiously, Shreddy crept away from the array of portals, keeping so low to the hard ground that his stripy belly dragged in the dirt.

Auto-tuned laughter echoed through the cavern, and

bursts of colorful light bounced off of the rocky walls. A spotlight shone in a perfect circle on Shreddy, throwing his cowering body into sharp relief.

"You can't hide, Cat." It was the voice of the animated dragon from the Red-Haired Woman's game on the Play-Cube. "You're in my realm now."

Shreddy's fur fluffed.

"What do you want, Cat?"

Shreddy pressed his body against the ground, but he couldn't will himself to melt into the dirt. He looked up at the dragon.

Emerald wings, ruby eyes, and belly scales that shimmered like mother of pearl. The dragon had been hidden in the shadows, but now dancing spotlights glittered off of her Technicolor body. She looked magnificent, but she was nothing more than a lowly leech, draining the life away from all the PlayCube players in the neighborhood.

"*Leech*," Shreddy murmured under his whiskers.

"What was that?" the dragon bellowed, her voice climbing to an unreasonable auto-tuned pitch.

"You're a leech," Shreddy said. "You've been draining my human's life away. And I want it back."

The dragon chuckled, her mother-of-pearl belly swelling with the laughter. "Brave cat," she said.

Shreddy didn't feel brave, only right.

"I can't give your human's life back. I need it for my hoard." The dragon swung her giant tail, covered in cobalt spikes, to gesture at a pile of gold coins heaped against the cavern's far wall. "Go, look at them."

Shreddy didn't move.

"Go!" the dragon roared. "Look at how beautiful my gold coins are!"

Terrified, Shreddy scurried across the cavern to the pile

of coins. Shivering in terror, he stammered at the giant dragon watching his every move, "Yes, they're... very shiny." She seemed mollified.

The dragon reached one of her talons down and daintily grabbed a single coin between two of her silver claws. "This one belongs to your human."

Shreddy saw a number inscribed on the coin—23. He looked back at the pile of coins and saw that they all had different numbers. "What does the number mean?"

"The more life that a human gives me, the higher the number. Also, the more valuable." The dragon sneered, showing her topaz teeth, and tossed the Red-Haired Woman's coin back on the pile. "Twenty-three isn't very good. Your human is pathetic."

"If it's not valuable, then let me take it."

"Valuable or not, it's mine!" The tone of the dragon's voice jumped all over, not restraining itself to a single octave. Tendrils of smoke escaped her nostrils. She shifted her emerald wings. Then she said, "However, I will dance you for it."

Confused, Shreddy asked, "*Dance* me for it?"

"You've watched me dance! I've seen you!" the dragon shouted. "Don't play dumb, Cat."

Shreddy hadn't paid much attention to the rules of the PlayCube game. He did remember the dragon dancing though. She looked ridiculous.

"Cats don't dance," he said.

"Do cats squish if you step on them?"

Shreddy considered his options. They mostly involved twining tentacle-cords and stomping dragon feet. "All right. I'll dance."

A distortion-heavy metal-rock bossa nova song rang through the cavern, drilling its way into Shreddy's spine.

The dragon swayed her tail, shuffled her talons, and flapped her wings—seemingly to three different beats. The air around her exploded in fireworks. She pirouetted looking more like a child's top than a ballerina. Yet flowers and a banner reading, "OUTSTANDING!", fell from the dark ceiling of the cavern.

Shreddy tried to sway to the beat, but all he managed was an irritable tail-twitch.

The dragon pirouetted again, and two more banners fell for her.

Shreddy turned in a few circles, pretending for his dignity that he was settling down for a nap rather than *dancing*, but nothing fell from the ceiling for him.

The song ended in a hideous blare of brass.

A rainbow arched over the dragon, and her auto-tuned laughter filled the cavern. "I won, Cat. Play again?"

Shreddy grumbled.

"What was that?" she roared. "You want me to find out whether cats burn if I breathe fire on them?"

Shreddy danced again. And again. By the fifth contest, he'd worked himself up to shifting his weight from one paw to the other and swishing his tail. By the fifteenth, he raised himself to standing on his back paws and did a little jig, earning himself a banner that read, "NICE!"

By the twentieth contest, Shreddy realized that the dragon was sucking his life away just like the Red-Haired Woman's. He would dance in this torture chamber until he died. He'd never sleep on the Red-Haired Woman's bed again, feel her idle caress in the early morning, or sit on her lap. He was doomed to be an animated, dancing fool, two-dimensional on her TV screen.

Shreddy couldn't take it anymore. Let the dragon burn

him, squash him, or strangle him with white tentacle cords. Anything was better than this.

Shreddy ran for the portal home to his living room.

The music stopped.

Deathly silence.

In a small, high voice, the dragon said, "Don't you want to save your game?"

"God no!" Shreddy yowled, ready to leap into the swirling portal.

"Are you sure?" The dragon sounded so sad.

Shreddy twisted one ear to the side, intrigued. "I'm sure," he said. "Delete my game."

The dragon sighed, steam rising from her nostrils. Then she lumbered over to her pile of gold coins, lifted a single coin, and flipped it into the air. It twirled, arcing through the cavern and plopped into a well of lava on the far side.

Shreddy blinked in surprise. "Delete *all* games," he said.

"No!" the dragon wailed, her voice tripping up and down a dozen octaves. Yet, she picked up another coin.

THE TENTACLE CORDS lay as lifeless as calamari on the living room floor. Shreddy napped smugly on the couch.

Cooper and Susie came tearing in with as much energy as if they hadn't spent the afternoon playing fetch and chase at the dog park. Susie jumped onto the couch, crowding into Shreddy's space. The Red-Haired Woman followed her, grabbing the knobby PlayCube controller off the floor on her way.

"Ew," she said. "Why is this sticky?"

Cooper slobbered the honey off of the PlayCube, despite the Red-Haired Woman's protests. She cleaned the honey off of the controller with a tissue. Then she tried to start her game.

"What the hell? Level one? I was on level twenty-three!" She pulled her smartphone out of her pocket, touched the screen, and then held it to her ear. "Hey, Tony, are you having trouble with *Dance, Dance, Dragon?*"

Shreddy heard the voice in the phone say, "I emailed customer support. They said it was an irrecoverable server crash. A complete wipe of the system. Everyone's saved games were lost."

"Damn."

"I know. Want to play *Space Blazer Online?*"

Shreddy's ears perked up. He loved watching the tiny spaceships fly around the Red-Haired Woman's computer screen when she played *Space Blazer Online*. And the best part was there was no room for Susie or Cooper on her desk chair.

But there was plenty of room in her lap for a brave, dragon-defying cat.

6

SHREDDY AND THE CARNIVOROUS PLANT

SHREDDY WAS a tabby cat who liked to chew on plants. In the distant, glorious past, his owner had kept orchids in her kitchen window. These days, though, the Red-Haired Woman kept the house empty of plants. Shreddy had to roam the neighborhood, sampling the grasses, weeds, flowers, and herbs in other house's gardens to get his fix of greens. His favorites were parsley, sage, thyme, and, of course, catnip.

Then the Red-Haired Woman brought home a Venus flytrap.

"Check it out, Shreddy," she said, displaying the strange toothy plant in a small terracotta pot. "This will help get rid of that fly you keep chasing." She set it on the kitchen counter, beside the sink.

Shreddy liked chewing on plants. He wasn't so sure he liked the idea of plants who did their own chewing. Besides, he loved batting at the fly that had been trapped in the kitchen. He chose not to catch it *on purpose*.

Still, the Red-Haired Woman's assumption that he'd leave the Venus flytrap alone proved accurate. Shreddy sat on the kitchen counter, twitching his tail and staring at the flytrap for a long time after the Red-Haired Woman went off to play her computer games. But, when he finally approached close enough to sniff it, the long-toothed clamshell of a plant smelled wrong. Putrid, decaying. It was nothing Shreddy wanted in his mouth. Or on the kitchen counter.

Shreddy raised a paw to strike the terracotta pot, dash it to the floor, but the long green teeth and the sinister redness inside the plant's mouth gave him pause. He stayed his paw. This wasn't a plant he wanted to cross.

Besides, it was the Red-Haired Woman who'd offended him by bringing such an unappetizing plant into his kitchen. Shreddy settled on a different plan: let the plant live, but punish the Red-Haired Woman.

He started by knocking the salt and pepper shakers to the floor. Then he ripped open a bag of gummy bears. He had no interest in eating the sugar-sweet confections, so he usually left them alone. Thus the Red-Haired Woman didn't bother hiding bags of them in the refrigerator like she did the stash of catnip. This would teach her.

Shreddy surveyed his work. It wasn't enough—he knocked the salt and pepper shakers on the floor almost every day; a shredded bag of gummy bears was nothing. He needed to show the Red-Haired Woman that she'd crossed a line. He needed to show her that a toothy plant was a bad idea. He needed to feed it something she valued.

Shreddy trotted purposefully into the computer room where he saw the Red-Haired Woman sitting at her desk with both dogs, Cooper the Labradoodle and Susie the Cavalier King Charles Spaniel, curled up at her feet. She was playing *Space Blazer Online*, completely absorbed in the flashy graphics on her computer screen. The dogs were snoring.

Perfect. No one would notice when Shreddy slipped over to the little bowl of USB drives and stole one. It would serve her right to have one of her precious USB drives chomped to bits by the scary looking little plant. Shreddy chose a plastic pink USB drive labelled "AI lab backup," because it looked particularly shiny. He grabbed it in his teeth and trotted back to the kitchen.

Cautiously, Shreddy prowled across the kitchen counter, stalking the bizarre plant. Finally, he pounced, jumping close enough to drop the pink USB drive into the flytrap's toothy maw.

The green mouth snapped shut. It was barely big enough to close over the USB drive.

Startled, Shreddy jumped backwards and fell off the kitchen counter.

He did not land on his feet.

Grumpy and sore, Shreddy waddled off to the Red-Haired Woman's bed to take a nap. He curled up on the foot of the bed and gleefully awaited the Red-Haired Woman's shrieks when she discovered that one of her USB drives had been fed to her nasty old plant. He fell asleep waiting.

SHREDDY AWOKE in the wee hours of the morning. The Red-Haired Woman was under the covers, and the dogs were sprawled beside her, snoring again. But there was another sound in the air, a crinkling sound almost too soft to hear.

Shreddy tilted his head and turned his ears. The sound was coming from the kitchen. Irritated and curious,

Shreddy got up from his cozy warm spot on the comforter and followed the crinkling sound.

From the far side of the kitchen, Shreddy saw with his night vision the Venus flytrap on the counter. The plant drooped over the edge of its terra cotta pot. No, wait, it was *reaching* down over the edge, nipping at the raggedy plastic pouch of gummy bears that Shreddy had ripped open. The pouch wasn't quite in its reach.

It had no right to move like that. Plants are supposed to hold still. Furious, Shreddy raced across the kitchen, jumped up onto the counter, and hissed at the little plant, spitting and snarling.

The wide toothy mouth of the Venus flytrap halted its nipping. Then it turned slowly toward Shreddy, almost as if it were looking at him.

Shreddy shivered, and the fur along his spine fluffed up. His tail brushed out. He hissed again.

The little plant held still for a moment. Then it did droop, laying its strange toothy mouth of a head on the soil in its pot. The little plant looked so sad and hopeless, it intrigued Shreddy. Curiosity got the better of him, and he reached a paw out to the pouch of gummy bears. He pushed the pouch a little closer. He wanted to see what the plant would do with them.

Shreddy waited. His tail twitched. The plant did nothing.

Impatient and tired, Shreddy wondered if he'd been imagining things and should go back to the Red-Haired Woman's bed...

The Venus flytrap chomped its mouth as if it were tasting the smell of gummy bear on the air. It lifted its toothy head and reached for the gummy bears again. This time, its long, sharp green teeth pierced a yellow bear. The mouth clamped down hard on the artificially lemon flavored confection. Chomp, chomp, chomp. The tiny plant ate every gummy bear, a rainbow of sugar sweets, within its reach. Suddenly, it didn't look scary or wrong. It looked cute and funny, eager and delighted.

Shreddy chuckled. He sat back on his haunches and curled his tail around himself. "I think I'll call you Sweet Tooth," he said. He wondered what else he could feed the little plant.

Shreddy didn't see anything else suitable on the counter, so he pawed open one of the cupboards. There was a bag of foil wrapped toffees—perfect. Shreddy knocked it down to the counter, tore into the plastic bag with his teeth, and then batted the shiny toffee squares within reach of Sweet Tooth one by one.

He chuckled each time Sweet Tooth chomped into a toffee, foil-wrapping and all. It was vicariously satisfying, feeding his funny new pet plant.

Eventually, Shreddy ran out of toffees. At about the same time, he tired of the game. Shreddy knocked the empty plastic packaging onto the floor where the Red-Haired Woman would blame the dogs for eating the sweets.

Then he wished Sweet Tooth good night and went back to the Red-Haired Woman's bed.

THE NEXT DAY, Sweet Tooth looked bigger, and there were pink speckles—the same color as the USB drive—on the green of its clamshell leaves. Yet, it showed no signs of the animation it had exhibited the night before. It stood eerily still, clamshell mouth clamped shut and held high.

Shreddy sat on the far side of the counter and watched Sweet Tooth carefully. He wasn't sure if he wanted confirmation that the last night hadn't been a dream, or if he simply wanted to see what the little plant might do next. Either way, he was fascinated.

He would have stayed on the counter all day, except the Red-Haired Woman kicked him off to cook dinner. She didn't like him hanging around the counter with the raw hamburger and bags of vegetables sitting out or when the burners on the stove were on.

Shreddy didn't mind staying away from the onions as she diced them, but he would have loved to lick the raw hamburger.

It was harder to see Sweet Tooth from the floor, but Shreddy could have sworn he saw the clamshell leaves turning slightly as if to smell the simmering hamburger, onions, and peppers. Shreddy found it hard to imagine Sweet Tooth being interested in onions or peppers. Plants eating plants? No. Sweet Tooth might be a carnivore, but a cannibal? It was much more likely that in addition to candy, Sweet Tooth had a taste for meat.

Shreddy couldn't steal ground hamburger for himself, let alone a pet plant. However, he might be able to steal the dog food, and their kibble smelled a lot like meat. Shreddy chuckled at the idea of Sweet Tooth eating up the dog's food while they slept.

Shreddy liked the idea enough that after the Red-Haired Woman and the dogs went to bed, he brought a mouthful of the oily, yicky kibble up to the counter and spat it out beside Sweet Tooth's terra cotta pot.

He sat back and watched as the little plant repeated its performance from the last night, gobbling down the dog food, one crunchy piece of kibble at a time.

Shreddy liked having a pet. He also liked having a secret. Every day, the Red-Haired Woman marveled at Sweet Tooth's growth, and the dogs bemoaned their less-than-full food dishes. Only Shreddy and Sweet Tooth knew why.

∽

IN ONLY A WEEK, Sweet Tooth doubled in size. The Red-Haired Woman repotted the Venus flytrap into a glazed green pot, much larger than the terra cotta one. Sweet Tooth looked much more comfortable with a little more room.

That night, Shreddy came out to feed his pet plant and found the Venus flytrap missing. The glazed pot was empty. Then Shreddy heard crunching from the direction of the dog bowls.

A trail of fresh potting soil led from the glazed pot, across the counter and down to the dog bowls. Dirt clung to Sweet Tooth's mess of thin roots, but its clamshell leaves chomped happily on the full bowl of kibble.

At first, Shreddy was delighted. The whole sight was hilarious—Cooper and Susie would have been incensed if they could see a Venus flytrap eating their food. As Sweet Tooth finished off the second bowl, however, Shreddy decided that things had gone too far. The Red-Haired Woman would surely notice if the dog bowls were completely empty, and she couldn't possibly miss the potting soil all over her counter.

Grumpily, Shreddy snapped at the funny plant, "Get back in your pot!"

Sweet Tooth's clamshell head turned to look at Shreddy, almost guiltily. The green clamshell leaves with their sharp, spiny teeth opened and closed a few times before finally forming the word, "Hungry."

Shreddy was startled that Sweet Tooth could talk, and he felt strangely bad about the idea of sending his pet plant back to its pot hungry. "You've eaten all the dog food," he said. Shreddy looked around the kitchen, but there wasn't much to offer Sweet Tooth. The cupboards were mostly filled with cans and boxes of useless, uncooked pasta. "All of the good food is in the refrigerator." He gestured toward the giant white box with his nose. "And I can't open it."

"*Open.*" Sweet Tooth's voice was high and reedy, but eerily commanding.

Shreddy didn't like being commanded. He was no dog.

"*Can't,*" Shreddy growled. He also didn't like to admit weakness, but opening the refrigerator was something he simply couldn't do. He had tried. When he was a kitten, he'd scrabbled at the heavy, white door with ineffectual claws. Kittens have less pride than cats.

While Shreddy glowered, the hungry Venus flytrap clambered across the linoleum floor on its many dirt-clad roots. It came to the Monolithic Trove of Taunting and lifted its foremost roots to feel the impenetrable white surface. The dirty tendrils roved over the clean flat front of the refrigerator until they came to the edge. Suddenly, Sweet Tooth reached with more of its roots, pushing itself root-first into the crack at the edge of the refrigerator's door.

Shreddy had clawed at that door. It didn't budge. He expected Sweet Tooth's efforts to be equally fruitless. He began to laugh at the little plant, but he had to swallow his chortles—Sweet Tooth may have been no larger than a kitten, but its roots had leverage that Shreddy's claws hadn't.

The door popped open.

Shreddy's eyes widened.

Holy catnip. The refrigerator was open.

Thinking of *catnip*... The refrigerator was where the Red-

Haired Woman kept it. Shreddy launched himself past Sweet Tooth, through the open gap into the refrigerator. He heedlessly knocked over red and yellow squeeze bottles and a glass jar filled with oblong green things. He crashed his way to the back of the refrigerator and found the folded up plastic baggy of dried catnip. Precious plastic baggy! Shreddy sank his teeth into the thin, translucent plastic, and the spicy, sweet smell of catnip made him shiver. Or maybe that was the refrigerator.

He carried the baggy back out to the kitchen proudly. It dangled from his mouth like a prize mouse, except infinitely more valuable.

While Sweet Tooth continued crashing about inside the refrigerator, Shreddy tore into the baggy. The sensuous confetti of dried catnip leaves spilled across the linoleum, and their smell intoxicated Shreddy. He looked at the tiny bits of leaf—they glowed like mouse eyes, daring him to catch them, and the linoleum under them warped and stretched. Shreddy's paws went numb. He couldn't stand anymore, so he rolled against the linoleum—it was so much smoother than he'd ever noticed!—and the floor cradled him like a hammock, rocking and rocking. Back and forth. Or maybe Shreddy was doing the rocking?

The sweet, spicy smell of catnip enveloped him. Shreddy could feel it filling him, swelling his body. His paws tingled, and, as they regained feeling, they grew large and blunt like Cooper's paws. His ears grew and flopped down on his head. The catnip had turned him into a dog! Shreddy didn't need to worry about his pride any more. He could be stupid and carefree as he pleased!

He bounded up onto his new dog paws, and he chased his brushy dog's tail in circles, laughing and barking like Susie had when she was a puppy.

Sweet Tooth emerged from the refrigerator with a plastic package of sliced salami in its clamshell mouth. Shreddy had never seen anything so normal in his life. He watched the little plant slither its way across the linoleum, up the cupboards—using their drawer pulls as a ladder—and back into its glazed pot.

Sweet Tooth was a god. The sage of catnip.

Shreddy fell asleep on the linoleum, paws in the air and flakes of dried leaf clinging to his fur.

SHREDDY AWOKE to warm dog breath and a wet nose nudging his face. Cooper's concerned brown eyes looked down at him. When Shreddy hissed and slashed the Labradoodle's nose, the dumb dog just woofed, "He's okay!"

Susie said, "Of course, he is." She'd seen Shreddy strung out on catnip before. Though, the Red-Haired Woman never gave him more than a pinch of it. Certainly not a whole bag.

"How'd you get it open?" Susie asked, looking at the disheveled refrigerator. She nosed through the mess of jars and bottles on the floor in front of it, but she found nothing good.

"You wouldn't understand," Shreddy hissed. He licked his fur, trying to put himself back in order. "It was far too clever for you."

Cooper jumped his front paws onto the bottom shelf of the barely-cold-anymore box and wagged his tail. "Master probably left it open."

Susie laughed.

Shreddy couldn't stand it when dogs laughed at him.

At least, when the Red-Haired Woman walked in,

wearing her morning robe and slippers, she gave Shreddy a glare that clearly blamed him for the disordered refrigerator and mess on the floor. She might not always have the best taste—bringing home Susie, Cooper, all sorts of haunted electronics, and now Sweet Tooth—but, at least, she understood that Shreddy was a criminal mastermind. She respected him.

And she knew how to keep him out of the refrigerator.

Later that day, she affixed an adhesive lock to the refrigerator door.

SWEET TOOTH STRAINED against the closed refrigerator door that night, roots writhing, to no avail.

"Hungry!" Sweet Tooth whined. The plant had already cleaned the dogs' bowls, and everything in the cupboards seemed to be canned or uselessly un-food-like.

"Here," Shreddy said, taking pity on the plant. "Follow me. I know where the Red-Haired Woman hides her dark chocolate." He couldn't open the desk drawer himself, but after seeing Sweet Tooth's work on the refrigerator, he had no doubt that Sweet Tooth could.

The Red-Haired Woman kept a one-pound bar of eighty-six percent cacao chocolate in her top desk drawer. She would chip away at it, slowly eating the chocolate over the course of months.

Sweet Tooth ate the whole bar in five minutes.

The next morning, the Red-Haired Woman found the empty wrapper on the floor under her desk with horror. She knew Shreddy couldn't eat that much chocolate, and she could never have imagined the truth.

"Cooper! Susie!" she screamed. The dogs came running,

happy to hear their names. The Red-Haired Woman grabbed their faces, each in turn, pried their mouths open, and said, "You stupid, stupid dogs! Which one of you ate this?" There was no chocolate smell on either of the dogs' breath, so she had no choice: she rushed both of them to the vet.

THE NEXT THREE days were quiet. Shreddy enjoyed having the dogs gone. He didn't know why the Red-Haired Woman looked so sad when she told him that the vet wanted to keep them on fluids for seventy-two hours to be safe.

During the days, Shreddy slept on the Red-Haired Woman's lap as she played games on her computer. At night, Shreddy took Sweet Tooth out mousing. The little plant—now big—had outgrown the sources of food that could be stolen in the Red-Haired Woman's house. It had even opened and emptied the sugar, flour, and corn meal jars. Sweet Tooth had eaten the sugar and corn meal. The flour was dumped on the floor.

It was time to teach Sweet Tooth how to hunt and feed itself.

Of course, Shreddy was terrible at mousing, so he didn't so much teach as pounce around the backyard, failing to catch mice, followed by Sweet Tooth. Eventually, Sweet Tooth got the idea. With all those grabby roots and the disarming appearance of a plant, Sweet Tooth made a *much* better mouser than Shreddy did.

Shreddy found it hilarious to watch Sweet Tooth sneak up on unsuspecting mice, wrap its roots around them, and then gobble them up with its clamshell shaped mouth.

Stupid mice.

Funny plant.

When the dogs came home, their heads hung low, and their ears drooped. Shreddy laughed at first, but it unnerved him the way that they slunk around the house, wiggling nervously any time the Red-Haired Woman looked at them or petted them.

"I'm sorry! I'm sorry!" Susie woofed at the Red-Haired Woman. "Whatever it was that I did, I won't do it again!"

Cooper just whined, "Love, love, love you," to her and leaned his whole body into her scritches like they were a rare resource he might never experience again.

Shreddy hated feeling guilty.

So, he also didn't like it when Sweet Tooth came to him that night to say, "*Hungry.*"

"Go mousing," Shreddy admonished, hoping that his pet plant wouldn't wake the Red-Haired Woman or the dogs also asleep on the bed. Surely, he'd done his part in feeding Sweet Tooth. The giant Venus flytrap should be able to care for itself now.

"No mice," Sweet Tooth said, shoving its toothy clamshell head against Shreddy's side.

Shreddy didn't like the feel of needly plant-teeth combing his fur.

"Ate all the mice," Sweet Tooth said.

Suddenly, Shreddy realized just how big Sweet Tooth's mouth had become.

It was as big as him.

And it didn't look cute and funny any more.

Shreddy's fur fluffed out, and his claws extended. He jumped onto his feet and arched his back. "You're... hungry?" he said guardedly. Hopefully, the blind plant couldn't sense and understand his body language through the vibrations on the bed.

"*Hungry*," Sweet Tooth confirmed. The Venus flytrap raised its clamshell head and tilted it as if listening.

The room was quiet.

Except for the panting, snuffling, breathing of the dogs. And the quieter breathing of the Red-Haired Woman.

"Dog... food?" Sweet Tooth asked.

Since Sweet Tooth's escapades had begun, the Red-Haired Woman had taken to storing the bags of dog and cat food in the locked garage. "I can't get you any more dog food," Shreddy said.

"Dog..." Sweet Tooth began but trailed off, smacking its clamshell mouth.

Shreddy imagined waking the Red-Haired Woman and making a run for it while Sweet Tooth ate Cooper and Susie.

They'd start over, find a new house, one without annoying dogs or a giant carnivorous plant in it. But Shreddy knew the Red-Haired Woman better than that. She'd never leave her dogs behind. Shreddy would have to save them from Sweet Tooth too.

He had to get Sweet Tooth out of their house.

"You don't want to eat dogs," Shreddy said.

Cooper whined in his sleep, as if he'd heard Shreddy's words.

"Want to eat..." Sweet Tooth began.

Shreddy cut him off: "You want to eat..." He racked his brain for the best thing to eat—not *his* favorite, which was canned salmon, but the Red Haired Woman's favorite— "...chocolate fudge cake."

Sweet Tooth stopped smacking its clamshell mouth and started writhing its roots. Shreddy hoped that was a sign of interest.

"There's a bakery a few blocks away," Shreddy said. "I can lead you there."

Shreddy watched Sweet Tooth's roots writhe. They were mesmerizing like string or mouse tails. But dangerous like a boa constrictor or octopus tentacles. Shreddy shivered.

"You liked the chocolate, right? The bakery is full of chocolate—cakes and cookies and lots of chocolate. All kinds of chocolate." Shreddy had only walked past the bakery while roaming the neighborhood. He didn't really know what was in it, but he needed to lure Sweet Tooth away from his Red-Haired Woman and the dogs.

Sweet Tooth smacked its clamshell mouth again, and Shreddy cringed.

"Chocolate," Sweet Tooth said. "Show me."

Shreddy slunk off of the bed and crept through the house, belly close to the floor and ears flat. He wanted to hide, and he hated knowing that a mouth as big as him— and hungry—was following behind.

Sweet Tooth could barely cram itself through the pet door anymore. *When had the plant gotten bigger than the dogs?* All the way through the darkened streets, Shreddy wished that a big dog or a human would see the hideous parade of a ravenous Venus flytrap following a scared tabby and come rescue him. He'd never wished for a big dog before.

No one came to rescue Shreddy.

He came to the windowed storefront that read "Bakery" in silver letters decorated with gold flourishes. He could see the rows of cakes on pedestals behind the glass. Some of them were definitely chocolate.

"In there," Shreddy meowed.

Sweet Tooth stood eerily still. Then the flytrap launched itself at the window and beat the glass with thick gnarly roots. It snapped at the glass with its clamshell, as ineffectual as Shreddy's tiny kitten claws had been against the refrigerator.

"You need a tool," Shreddy miewed, so quiet he could barely hear himself. But Sweet Tooth heard him, stopped beating the window, and turned to face the terrified cat. Shreddy closed his eyes. He couldn't look at the monster that he'd grown from a funny little plant. "A rock. Hit the window with a rock."

Sweet Tooth made a harrumphing sound and scrambled off to find a rock. Shreddy shrank into the shadows and watched Sweet Tooth gather rocks from the small parking lot beside the bakery.

Was this his opportunity to run? Or would running anger Sweet Tooth? Shreddy didn't know what the plant thought of him. Was it fond of him? Was he nothing more than a giant, eminently edible mouse?

He should have run. Shreddy felt sure of that. But he couldn't stop watching.

The glass shattered over Sweet Tooth, but the flytrap was unharmed. Alarm bells rang out. Sweet Tooth ignored the clanging racket and crawled over the stinging-sharp rubble, up into the bakery window.

In one bite, Sweet Tooth ate a chocolate cake decorated with pink flowers. In another bite, it ate a white cake covered in rainbow sprinkles. Then another chocolate one. And another.

It would have been funny if it weren't so scary.

Shreddy watched until a police car came, flashing red and blue. Then he high-tailed it home, through the pet door, and into the Red-Haired Woman's bedroom where he hid under the bed, miserable and too scared to sleep.

$\sim$

ALL NIGHT, Shreddy imagined Sweet Tooth eluding the cops and following him home. He only came out from under the bed in the morning to sit on the Red-Haired Woman's desk, beside her computer monitor, and paw at the news articles on her social networks, hoping she'd click on them.

She shoved him off the desk.

"Go sleep in a patch of sunlight or something," she said. Then she posted an update online saying, "My crazy cat won't leave my computer alone today!"

Shreddy jumped back up and tried pawing at her keyboard instead. The Red-Haired Woman posted the gibberish that he typed attributed to "Crazy Cat," but the only news articles she clicked on were about new PlayCube games—nothing local, nothing about a break-in at a bakery.

Shreddy had only known Sweet Tooth to move around at night. Like a vampire. So, he figured that he was safe while the sun was out. At least, he was safe from Sweet Tooth. When the Red-Haired Woman found Sweet Tooth's green glazed pot, now empty, she yelled, "I don't know how you got rid of a plant that big and healthy, Shreddy, but I know you did it!" Then she dug out a squirt gun.

As the day wore on, Shreddy's fur dried, and he found himself filled with conflicting emotions. He was used to mousing at night with Sweet Tooth, and he kept looking forward to that routine—only to feel disappointed, filled with fear, and also anger.

He missed Sweet Tooth.

Still, Shreddy was no fool. When the night finally came, he hid under the Red-Haired Woman's bed. Surely, if Sweet Tooth returned, the toothy plant would eat the dogs first— they were lolled out on top of the bed in plain sight, and they were much smaller and more bite-sized than the Red-

Haired Woman. Their yelps would warn Shreddy and the Red-Haired Woman, giving them time to escape while Cooper and Susie served as a noble sacrifice. Dogs liked being noble, right?

Tentacle-like roots did not creep across the bedroom floor. But Shreddy heard the flapping of the pet door across the house. It didn't flap once like it should. It kept flapping and flapping.

Finally, Shreddy's curiosity got the better of him, and he crept out from under the bed. He stuck close to the walls, moving like a stripey shadow.

"Here kitty, kitty!" Sweet Tooth called in its reedy voice, a hideous mocking mimicry of the way that the Red-Haired Woman called Shreddy.

The sound sent tingles down Shreddy's spine, all the way to the tip of his fluffed out tail. He hissed. "Go away, Demonic Satan Plant!" Yet, his curiosity kept pulling him across the house toward the flapping pet door.

Shreddy got close enough to see the pet door through the dark: Sweet Tooth's roots crammed through the door, reaching and straining; then they withdrew, and Sweet Tooth's clamshell mouth poked partway through. It didn't fit. Sweet Tooth had grown too large for the pet door and could only fit partway through at a time.

"Here kitty, kitty!" Sweet Tooth called again.

Shreddy left a safe distance between him and the pet door. His tail swished. "What do you want? You've eaten all the food here."

"Cat..." Sweet Tooth said. "Food."

All of Shreddy's cold fear boiled into anger. "No!" he yowled. "Cat not food! How dare you! After everything I did for you?"

Sweet Tooth's clamshell mouth withdrew from the pet door, and a gnarly root tip reached through. The root tip dropped a ball, small enough to fit in the Red-Haired Woman's hand, that landed on the floor with a soft thud. It smelled like sugar. And cream.

Was Sweet Tooth trying to lure Shreddy into its tentacley grasp with bakery confections?

The root tip broke open the pastry ball. It was a cream puff, filled with sweet, sweet, milky cream. Shreddy wanted it, but he prepared to sneer at the false gift anyway. Then the root tip batted the broken cream puff away from the pet door. It skidded across the linoleum floor, right into Shreddy's paws.

He jumped, startled. Thankfully, he jumped backward, away from the root reaching through the pet door. Regardless, the root withdrew, and Sweet Tooth's clamshell mouth shoved itself back into view.

"Cat food," Sweet Tooth said.

Shreddy sniffed the cream puff, tentatively re-evaluating Sweet Tooth's words. He licked the cream. It was heavenly.

"Thank cat," Sweet Tooth said.

Shreddy kept licking the cream until every crevice of the pastry was clean of the delicious white custard. His voice dropped down low, and Shreddy said, "You're welcome."

The massive Venus flytrap withdrew from the pet door, and it flapped shut. Shreddy stared at the closed door for a long time. Finally, he went to sleep on the Red-Haired Woman's bed, full of cream and free of fear.

THE NEXT DAY, Shreddy saw a link to a news article on the Red-Haired Woman's computer titled, "*Is There a Cake Thief?*

Mysterious Bakery Break-Ins!" The Red-Haired Woman didn't click on it, but the title was enough. Shreddy knew that his pet was okay. Sweet Tooth could take care of itself now.

And if the occasional cream puff or éclair appeared inside the pet door during the night? Well, that was just icing.

PART II

OTHER MAGICAL CATS

7

SONGS OF FISH AND FLOWERS

PINK ROSES TWISTED THEIR PETALS, soaking in the afternoon sun. Red begonias and calla lilies decorated the edges of the rose beds. And, Carly, a white-faced calico sunned herself in the grass, enjoying the subtle scent of mint, rosemary, and catnip that drifted to her on the gentle wind.

Carly had been a witch's cat but no longer; the garden had been the witch's garden but without her tender ministrations would soon fall to weeds, bracken, and brambles. Carly and the roses were orphaned when their kitchen witch disappeared. Neither cat nor roses knew the complex dramas of human life that could force a woman who loved them to leave. They didn't know why she had gone, only that she had.

"Well, roses, it's just us now," Carly meowed, alone in the garden. "The door doesn't open anymore." There were no loving hands to pet her. Carly looked through the windows, but the kitchen witch's house stayed resolutely dark inside. Carly used to sit on the kitchen witch's lap and sing her songs about fish. She had slept on soft pillows. Now she slept on the grass outside and sang to the roses.

Carly learned to roam the neighborhood, stealing food from other cats' bowls and gaining scritches, when she missed them, from other cats' owners. Though, they weren't the same as her witch's caresses. It was a wet summer, and the roses grew wild without the taming touch of the kitchen witch's clippers. As the garden grew wild, so did Carly's heart.

"Roses, sing with me!" Carly sang, one day when the sun beat down on her fur, making her black splotches burn with heat and the pupils in her golden eyes narrow to the merest slits. She blinked her sun-dazzled eyes, surprised to see that, though the roses didn't sing, they changed color.

They'd always been pink roses before. Now the blooms blushed red, orange, yellow, and violet. There were even blossoms of electric blue and crinkly white like old lace.

Carly smiled at the roses with her golden eyes. "You sing with colors." She sang with purrs, deep in her throat.

A year passed, and the For Sale sign on the house never moved. Carly grew used to her new feral nature, but she never forgot that she used to be a witch's cat and never stopped visiting the kitchen witch's garden to sleep in the grass and sing to the roses. Her life was different, but she didn't change.

The roses, however, changed every time she visited them.

Often their colors shifted like the rainbow sheen on an oil-slicked puddle. Sometimes they were shaped like fish. Once they jumped off of the bushes and ran around the grass like little fairies.

Then, one day, everything seemed normal. Carly sat in the middle of the overgrown, brittle and brown grass of the lawn; she twisted her ears about, disturbed and trying to understand how her magical garden had become as pedestrian as every other yard she visited.

"Why don't you sing?" she cried to the roses. She didn't care if they sang with their colors or their shapes or by twirling about the lawn around her, but she couldn't stand them staring at her like dead eyes. The pink roses, void of life and animation, became mere plants that had never belonged to a witch.

"Sing with me! Oh, please," her meowing voice fell to a sad whisper, "come back and sing with me."

Droplets of rain, small and erratic, tickled at Carly's whiskers; her back twitched at their touch. The droplets grew larger, heavier, and steadier. Carly crept under one of the rose bushes, thick and tangled from a year without pruning, to hide from the rain. She watched the water drench the parched ground and thought about all the comfortable hideouts throughout the neighborhood where she'd be better protected from the growing storm.

The woodpile behind the green house was always dry; the yellow house had a roaring machine behind it that vented warm air; and the children's playhouse behind the gray house had a comfortable child-sized chair to sleep on. But Carly couldn't leave the witch's garden. Without the roses, she felt severed from the glimmer in her heart that knew she was a witch's cat. She wasn't any old stray.

She was a witch's cat, and this was a witch's garden. That magic could not whither away. She wouldn't let it.

Nimbus clouds darkened the sky, and rain roared against the leaves shielding Carly. Water dripped and drizzled down between the vines, wetting her fur, but Carly sang to her roses, begging them to bring their magic back to her.

Her soft purring song was drowned out by the storm.

Morning came, and Carly's heart broke with the breaking of the clouds. Golden light graced the horizon, but the light in Carly's golden eyes dimmed.

She had imagined it all. She realized that now. The roses didn't dance and sing. There had probably never been a kitchen witch. She was a lonely stray, and that was all she had ever been.

"I'm ready to sing with you now." The voice vibrated in the very vines around Carly. She twisted her head about, turning her ears every direction, looking for the source, but she saw nothing. Only overgrown rose vines, thick with thorns and leaves.

"Who are you?" Carly meowed.

"I'm your roses." The voice sounded closer. As Carly stared into the vines, her eyes made out shapes—the curve of a muzzle, the straight line of whiskers. She blinked, but the vision only became clearer. A cat's face, drawn in rose vine with pink blossoms for eyes, stared down at her, smiling.

Carly cried out in joy, and her cry turned into the meowly growl of her favorite fish song. The ethereal cat face drawn in rose vines sang with her, and their duet was as sweet as morning dew on pink petals.

"You've never talked to me before," Carly said when the song was over.

"You've never needed me to," the rose vine cat answered, his muzzle distorting and twisting the rose bush as it moved.

Carly and the rose vine cat talked together for hours. She told him about the other cats and gardens in the neighborhood—she mostly didn't like the cats, and the gardens trended towards utilitarian plants like squash, zucchini, and tomatoes. Carly loved the yard that grew catnip but otherwise felt the gardens lacked beauty.

Then they reminisced together about their kitchen witch. At night, their witch had lit candles around her house, and the roses had seen them twinkle in the windows like stars on Earth. During the day, she had drawn patterns on the grass, sprinkling a special dust mixed from oatmeal and Italian spices. She'd drawn stars and circles, and she sat inside them, cross-legged and sang songs. Her songs weren't about fish but trees and gods and meadows and the sky. Silly songs that made no sense to roses or cats. Carly missed them anyway.

When the sun touched the horizon, blazoning the sky orange and pink, Carly's stomach, which had rumbled quietly for hours, began to growl in earnest. "If I go away to find food, will you still talk to me when I come back?"

The rose vine cat wouldn't answer, but Carly had to leave anyway. Her stomach commanded it.

From then on, Carly never knew what form to expect the rose vine to take when she visited. Some days, it was a normal rose vine; other days it sang with her as before; but, on the best days, the vines shaped themselves into the likeness of a cat and talked to her.

She hadn't known how lonely she'd become until the rose vine cat's company relieved her.

Fall approached and the rose bushes blossomed less frequently. "Will you still talk to me in the winter?" Carly asked the rose vine cat. "What will your eyes be when you have no more roses?"

"Closed, I suppose. I'll sleep through the winter, hibernate like a bear."

The answer made Carly sad, but it didn't surprise her. She was surprised, however, when the For Sale sign—so long in front of the kitchen witch's house—disappeared. She sniffed the rectangular hole in the ground where its wooden stake had stood for more than a year. Moist, bare soil like a wound in the Earth housed a single, wriggling worm. If it was an hallucination, it was a very good one.

Instead of jumping the fence and returning to her rose garden, Carly sat on the front drive and stared at the house. She imagined the windows lit again. She imagined people —different people than her kitchen witch—living inside. Her imaginings filled her with trepidation.

Would they cut back her roses? Would they tear out the precious bushes and plant horrible squash or pumpkins? Carly didn't want to sing to pumpkins or zucchini. She loved her roses.

Carly leapt over the eight-foot-tall fence, returning to her secret, overgrown garden of roses. The bushes had strong stems with twisting vines, but the leaves were sparser now that autumn kissed the air. Only two pink blossoms, past their prime and sloppy with petals ready to fall out, were left.

"Oh, my love! Run away with me! The witch's house has sold, and I don't know what the new people will do with you when they move in." The eight-foot-tall fence would no longer protect him.

The pink blossoms shuddered and winked; at different heights, on adjacent but separate bushes tangled together, the blossoms made for a skewed, cockeyed face. Vines rearranged themselves, drunkenly forming into the smiling cat face that Carly so loved.

"Run away?" the rose vine cat asked. "I'm rooted; I can't run."

Carly meowled in pain as if thorns cut her paw pads and tore at her sides. "What will I do without you?"

The rose vine cat whispered comforting words to Carly, but all his words were words of uncertainty: they didn't know if new people would move into the house; they didn't know if people would cut back the rose bushes; they didn't know.

The words of comfort rose and fell in tone, found a tune, and became a song. As the rose vine cat sang to Carly, he wrapped her in vines and leaves, caressing and cradling her, carefully protecting her from any thorns. She felt like a flower in his vines. Her heart, body, and soul opened to him like a rose spreading its petals to the sun. She found comfort in him, and he found release in her. They were not a rose garden and a cat, separate beings, but a rose garden cat, a singular creature unto itself complete.

Night came, and a gentle rain sprinkled the Earth like pinpricks of starlight sprinkled the breaks between the clouds in the sky. Carly awoke with the dawn, curled up on the hard dirt beneath her rose bush. No sign showed the magic that had taken place in the night, but Carly felt a change within her.

A SOLD sign succeeded the For Sale sign. Within a matter of days, trucks came. Doors that had stood shut for a year flapped open, letting people who carried sofas and lamps, bookcases and computer desks, in and out all day long. The gate in the eight-foot-tall fence that had protected Carly's rose garden swung wide, opening that secret place to the world.

Human children—a toddling boy and a curly-haired girl who babbled at anyone who listened, human or not—invaded the private garden. The girl picked the last two roses, and gave one to her toddling brother, keeping the other for herself.

Carly watched it all, perched safely out of reach on top

of the fence. She didn't mourn the roses. They would grow again.

For months, Carly held herself separate from the new family that lived in her home, but she felt a growing fondness for the young girl. Skeptically, Carly watched the family fill the house's windows with light—not candlelight like the witch's but artificial—fluorescent, halogen, the blue glow of computer screens, and the red and green twinkling of LEDs.

The most interesting light was the one that glowed under the covers in the little girl's room at night and peeked out at the edges of her blanket when she disappeared underneath with a book. The kitchen witch had read books when she sat on her rocking chair; she'd never read them under blankets.

Autumn deepened into winter. The rose bushes bore nothing but bare brambles, and Carly craved the warmth inside her witch's house. She wanted to sleep on that glowing blanket and pounce on the shape that moved under it. Carly let the new family take her in.

The toddling boy grabbed at Carly's tail and whiskers; the curly-haired girl squeezed her around the middle, carried her from room to room, and dressed her in doll clothes. The girl didn't let Carly sleep on her glowing blanket; she pulled the reluctant cat right underneath the covers with her. In spite of herself, Carly purred.

All through the winter, Carly's body grew thicker. She grew fat from the food her new family fed her, and her belly swelled with the pollen from her rose bush. She bore kittens in late December.

When the adult humans who lived in her home tore out the rose bushes in the spring to plant a vegetable garden, Carly didn't mourn. She had a new, young witch who brought magic to everything she saw. And she had her flowers—five kittens as perfect as roses. The adults may have seen perfectly ordinary kittens, but Carly and the girl knew better.

Carly saw dancing colors in her kittens' eyes and sang them songs of fish and flowers.

8

KATELYNN THE MYTHIC MOUSER

JENNA WAS ALMOST asleep when she felt the weight of a cat plop onto the end of her bed. She turned on the lamp on the bedside table and saw Katelynn, her aunt's dirt-brown tabby, sitting on the bed's patchwork comforter.

A tiny mouse hung by its tail from Katelynn's mouth, twisting and squirming, desperate to get away.

"Oh! Katelynn, thank you!"

Jenna crawled out of bed and hurried to set up her candles on the dresser beside the terrarium. She sprinkled salt and crumbled dried lavender. Then she opened her aunt's spell book to a page with an ornate drawing of Pegasus and an illusion spell handwritten in cramped, cursive letters.

"Okay, Katelynn, I'm ready. Don't let it get away."

The brown tabby jumped off the bed, trotted across the room, and then leapt delicately onto the dresser. Jenna lifted the mesh lid of the terrarium, and Katelynn dropped the terrified mouse inside.

Jenna and Katelynn watched the mouse cower, too

afraid to explore its new home. The other inhabitants of the terrarium, however, came out from their cardboard and colorful-plastic hiding places, drawn by curiosity—first, a perfect little unicorn as white as lily petals; then a serpentine, winged dragon as black as the night sky; and, finally, a golden-furred griffin with a tufted tail and clacky beak. Each creature was exactly the size of a mouse.

Jenna chanted the words from the spell book, just as her aunt had taught her to. The light from the candles grew taller, stretching up from the wicks and curling through the air like glowing smoke. The threads of light tangled in the air, sewing themselves up into the glowing image of Pegasus. Jenna finished chanting and blew the candles out, severing the illusion from them.

For a moment, the illusory Pegasus hung in the air. Then it condensed into a point of light and danced like a will-o-the-wisp into the terrarium. Finally, it landed on the cowering mouse's forehead, transforming the mouse into a downy, white pegasus, a perfect match for the unicorn.

Jenna grabbed Katelynn and hugged her around her furry middle. "I didn't think you'd catch the last mouse in time!"

Purrs overflowed the brown tabby, as if Jenna had squeezed them out of her.

Jenna put Katelynn back on the dresser and then swept off the salt and lavender into a trash bin. She reached to close the spell book, but Katelynn batted at her hand playfully.

"I'll play with you tomorrow, Katelynn, before my parents come to take me home."

Jenna had spent the summer at her aunt's house, learning magic. Her parents didn't know about the magic.

They just wanted her out of the way while they finished up their big, boring work project.

Jenna pulled her hand away from the book, and Katelynn pounced on the yellowed pages. She nosed and pawed, flipping through the pages, until the book lay open to the illusion for Hydra.

Katelynn sat proudly by the emerald green illustration of a serpent with many, many hissing heads. Aunt Molly said that Katelynn sometimes played with snakes in the yard. Unlike mice, she was never able to catch them. She'd opened the spell book to this page before.

"All right," Jenna said. "If you catch me one more mouse, I'll make a hydra. But, you'd better do it tonight. I'm leaving in the morning."

JENNA WOKE up to Katelynn pawing her face. It was still dark, but, as her eyes adjusted, Jenna made out the shape of another squirming mouse hanging only inches from her face.

"Ugh! Katelynn! Get that away from me."

Having been properly acknowledged, the brown tabby jumped off the bed, crossed the room, and leapt onto the dresser again. She pawed at the lid of the terrarium, catching the mesh in her claws.

Jenna laughed. "Silly cat." But she got out of bed and did all the work of casting an illusion spell again.

IN THE MORNING, Jenna woke to find Katelynn still on the

dresser, staring intently at the tiny, mythical creatures inside her terrarium. She'd never heard Katelynn purr so loudly.

The purring ended when Katelynn saw Jenna bring out her suitcase. As Jenna packed her clothes, Katelynn repeatedly hid in the suitcase and had to be dragged back out. When the suitcase was finally zipped shut, Katelynn yowled miserably.

"I told you that I have to go," Jenna said.

Katelynn skulked away and hid behind the terrarium.

Aunt Molly came to the door. "Are you all packed?" she asked.

Jenna looked around. With all her things packed back in her suitcase, the room looked like an ordinary guest room again, except for the terrarium filled with tiny, mythical creatures. "I guess so," she said. "I don't think Katelynn wants me to leave."

"I'm not surprised. She doesn't get much attention when you're not here."

Jenna couldn't help thinking about how sad Katelynn would be when she realized that the terrarium was leaving too. Aunt Molly had asked, and her parents had said it was okay for her to bring a terrarium filled with mice home. They wouldn't be able to see the illusion spells that turned them into a unicorn, dragon, griffin, hydra, and pegasus.

"I wish I could bring Katelynn with me..." Jenna felt bad as soon as she said it. Katelynn was her aunt's cat, not hers.

"Your mom said yes to mice—they stay in their terrarium. She wouldn't be okay with a cat."

The way Aunt Molly said it, she almost sounded like she would be okay with Jenna taking Katelynn. "Wouldn't you miss her?"

Aunt Molly shrugged. "She doesn't like me much. She

sleeps all day on the back of the couch and growls if I disturb her."

Katelynn was nothing like that for Jenna. She played with string, snuggled on the bed with her at night, and followed her all around the house. The idea of leaving Katelynn behind to be a grouchy, lonely cat was heartbreaking.

"What if..." Jenna thought about all the spells she'd learned that summer. They were mostly illusions, a few that could heat or cool water, and one that made her hair braid itself. But Aunt Molly knew many more. "Do you have a spell that could shrink Katelynn down to fit in my terrarium?"

Aunt Molly's brow furrowed in thought. "Maybe. Let me check."

Jenna followed Aunt Molly into her library room. All the walls were covered in book shelves, each shelf filled end to end with books. Even more books were stacked sideways on top of the others. There were two chairs, each with an end table beside it piled high in books, too. Jenna had spent a lot of time in the library room, but she hadn't been able to figure out any organization scheme to the books. Romance novels stood next to calculus text books. This year's best-sellers stood next to dusty old, handwritten spell books.

Aunt Molly walked around the room, putting her hand to a shelf occasionally, and finally pulled out one of the spell books. She flipped through the pages, settled on one, and said, "This would work. But I don't have time before your parents get here."

"Can I look?" Jenna nearly tripped over Katelynn who was weaving between her legs and purring. She picked the tabby up and crossed the room to look at Aunt Molly's open spell book.

The list of ingredients wasn't too hard—fresh mint, a

vial of peridot gems, thorns from the stem of an unopened rose, cinnamon incense, and almond oil. The chant looked difficult, much more difficult than any of the chants Jenna had done so far.

"Why don't you have time? We could do this right now," Jenna said.

"I can't just cast this on Katelynn. It doesn't only make an animal smaller—there has to be balance, so it makes another animal bigger."

"Maybe Katelynn could catch another mouse." Jenna smiled down at the tabby purring in her arms; golden cat eyes smiled up at her. "She's a terrific mouser."

"I don't want a giant mouse running around my house, thank you very much."

"A cat-sized mouse?" Jenna asked.

"No, probably just a rat-sized mouse, but I still don't want one." Aunt Molly shut the spell book and put it on one of the piles of books. "Tell you what, I'll figure something out, and I'll bring Katelynn to you in a few weeks."

Jenna didn't want to wait a few weeks. Katelynn wouldn't understand it was only a few weeks and would think Jenna had abandoned her. But Aunt Molly gave her the look that said, *this conversation is over*, and left the room.

Katelynn jumped out of Jenna's arms and batted the spell book off of the pile. It fell open on the floor, and Katelynn nosed it back to the page with the shrinking spell.

"Okay," Jenna said. "I won't give up, but if Aunt Molly says 'no mice,' then no mice. You'll have to catch something else."

Jenna went to the kitchen and got a vial of peridot gems, a small bottle of almond oil, and cinnamon incense from one of the spell supply drawers. She slipped the glass vial, bottle, and incense sticks in her pocket. Then she went outside to the garden, Katelynn following her.

When Jenna had first seen Aunt Molly's garden, it looked like a wild mess of greenery, an untamed jungle. But, over the summer, she'd learned to see the hidden structure —every plant was useful, and every inch of space was filled with plants.

Jenna waded her way between the waist-high lavender and rosemary shrubs to the brilliant green mint plants. She ripped off several sprigs, and their bright smell sharpened the air, overpowering all the other scents mingling together. Aunt Molly's garden always smelled amazing.

Aunt Molly had a rose bush of every color, each of them lost in a tangle of shrubs and herbs. They weren't for being beautiful; their blooms and thorns were for working spells.

Jenna made her way to the orange roses first, but all of the flowers were in wide bloom. She heard a rustling in the shrubs and looked down to see Katelynn with a mouse wriggling in her mouth.

"No mice," Jenna said.

Katelynn flattened her ears, dropped the mouse, and disappeared back into the greenery with her tail swishing angrily.

Jenna heard a car driving up the gravel road out front. That would be her parents. She needed to hurry.

The yellow and red roses were in full bloom too, but, on the white rose bush, she found a perfect, sweet little bud. Pressing her thumb against each thorn on its stem, she snapped them all off. She cradled the needle-sharp thorns carefully in the palm of her hand.

"Meow!" Katelynn snagged her claws in the fabric of Jenna's pants. Then she stared intently with her golden eyes at the rose bush.

Jenna followed her gaze: a tiny flutter of red-and-black wings landed on the edge of a rose leaf. A lady bug was small enough that Aunt Molly couldn't object to making it larger. Jenna gently picked up the ladybug and placed it in her thorn filled palm. She closed her hand loosely around the precious collection.

Back inside, Jenna fended off hugs from her parents and hurried into the guest room. Katelynn followed her like a shadow.

She locked the door, propped Aunt Molly's spell book against the terrarium, and began following its directions very precisely. She poured the green peridot gems out in a circle. She put the cinnamon incense in a censer and lit it. She arranged the rose thorns at the corners and intersections of an imaginary star inside the circle of peridot. She crushed the mint leaves, wadding it into a ball, and placed it at the center of the imaginary star.

Then she put a single drop of almond oil on the ladybug in her palm. Katelynn's nose wrinkled, but she let Jenna put a drop of almond oil in the fur between her ears.

Then Jenna took a deep breath and began chanting.

Nothing happened. Jenna worried that she'd got the pronunciation wrong, but she kept going, saying the words as clearly as she could.

Finally, she realized that the smell of mint and cinnamon was growing stronger, much stronger than anything she'd smelled before. The scent was so strong, it was as if she could see the green and red-brown color of the smells in the air.

The smell was sharp like peppermint. Then, suddenly, it was cool like spearmint.

Katelynn meowed. Her voice was much higher. Jenna felt giddy looking at the tiny mouse-sized cat on her dresser.

The lady-bug in her hand was the size of a quarter. She couldn't believe she'd pulled off such a difficult spell.

Katelynn jumped from the dresser onto Jenna's shoulder, purred, and bumped her head against Jenna's.

Knocking on the door. "Hey, Jenna, it's time to go," her mother said.

"Just a minute!" Jenna called. "I have to do one last thing."

Jenna cleaned up the supplies from the shrinking spell and set up the supplies for one last illusion spell. She ignored her parents knocking and complaints while she cast a reverse illusion on Katelynn—it didn't change how Jenna saw her, but her parents would see only another mouse.

Jenna let her impatient parents into the room. She held the ladybug out to Aunt Molly. "See this beetle I found?"

"That looks a lot like a ladybug," Aunt Molly said.

Jenna beamed with pride, and Aunt Molly shook her head knowingly.

"Couldn't wait two weeks, huh? Mind if I keep the ladybug? I mean, beetle. That might actually be my kind of pet."

"What are you talking about?" Jenna's father asked.

"Nothing," Jenna said, placing the giant ladybug in her aunt's palm. Then, turning to her mother, she said, "Look at my mice!"

Jenna showed her parents the terrarium. The pegasus and unicorn were racing each other around the edges. The griffin was preening her golden feathers. And the dragon flared her ebony wings, mock-fighting with the hissing emerald heads of the hydra.

Jenna's parents oohed appreciatively, almost as if they could really see.

"Okay, kiddo, let's get this circus out to the car," her mother said.

Her father said, "I'll carry your suitcase."

Before picking up the terrarium to take it to the car, Jenna placed her final mythical creature inside. She thought that Katelynn, a simple brown tabby cat, looked perfectly at home with the others. The smile in Katelynn's golden eyes agreed.

9

THE WHARF CAT'S MERMAID

THE SCRAGGLY WHITE KITTEN CROUCHED, trembling, behind the crates of fish. The smell was thick, but the scraps were thin. She'd been skittering from one stall to the next at Fisherman's Wharf all day, mewing for bits to eat. Few of the vendors favored her with more than a glance. One had chased her off with a broom.

Mari wasn't sure what had happened. Yesterday, she'd had a warm box to live in and littermates to cuddle with. The man who owned them had fed her and her littermates kibble and dangled a string for them to chase. Mari didn't know that the man had scrawled "KITT3NS $15" on the box, or that he'd given up on selling her. In only one day at the Wharf, all her littermates had sold, but she was a broken kitten. Her left back leg was deformed. She hopped to make up for it, and her limp didn't bother her. But it did mean that while her littermates sold for fifteen dollars apiece and went home with happy children, as souvenirs from Fisherman's Wharf, she'd been dumped out on the street. Left to fend for herself.

Mari scratched at the crate of fish, hoping to claw out a

piece of the delectable flesh she smelled inside. However, her claws were too small to rend the fish flesh effectively, and the fish were too large to pull out, unaltered, between the slats of the crate. She pressed her muzzle against the gap in the crate. The smell of the fish became nearly overpowering, but her teeth touched only splintery wood.

Frustrated, Mari hopped away from the crates. She continued on down the street, leaving the closed up stalls of the evening behind. She'd spent her first cold night and lonesome day as a street cat among the vendors of Fisherman's Wharf. It was time to move on.

Mari's mother had been a housecat, but she had told her kittens stories of catching mice and living free, as any self-respecting cat should. So, while Mari had no practical experience, she knew the basic idea behind surviving on the street. It was only a question of building up her mouse-catching skills before hunger overtook her.

If Mari had been a less patient kitten, she might have failed. As it was, the race between her slowly growing skills and her rapidly growing hunger was a close call. She hunted all night and day, stalking tiny, skittering prey. The second night, Mari was faint from hunger. Her paws felt like phantoms beneath her, and she was probably within an hour of laying down to rest—a rest that would have turned into the deep sleep of death. But the mouse she had stalked to its hole in the corner of a house's foundation emerged. Mari had waited so long and so patiently, the mouse was sure she had given up.

Claws against warm body and soft fur. The slap of her paw on the mouse's back felt so satisfying to Mari; she struck the dead mouse again and again. Finally, she settled to feast, discovering the pleasure of fresh mouse flesh and flavorful organs, including the tiny, stopped heart.

She savored that first mouse, but she learned quickly not to treat mouse flesh like a rare and valuable treat. It was the life blood she was to live on, and, as such, it had to become routine. A lot of things became routine for Mari—sleeping on cold, hard ground; hunting until her body was exhausted; and watching the people of the Wharf with a supreme loneliness. The occasional tourist would notice her, kneel down, and offer to give her head a scritch, but no degree of mewing motivated any of those people to pick her up and carry her home, whisking her away from the hard life of a stray.

Mari tried making friends with the other stray cats on the Wharf, but they were all much older than her and not very friendly. The black cat with the mangled ear—called Flamond by his ragtag gang of followers—hissed curses at her whenever she approached and instructed his gang to do the same. He believed her gimp leg was an omen of ill luck, and he didn't want her air of misfortune to rub off on him. He was ironically superstitious for a black cat.

The brown tabby, a loner, was more tolerant. She wouldn't speak to Mari, turning her nose away superciliously whenever Mari mewed to her. Mari didn't even know her name. However, she would let Mari approach her, and the two of them could share a silent hour or two, napping on the same sun-warmed square of concrete.

If Mari got too close, however, daring to press her shaking body against the motherly presence of the brown tabby's girth, then she found the end of the tabby's tolerance. As quick as a fat cat can, the brown tabby would leap to her feet and trot away, stomach swinging under her. Mari wondered how the tabby found enough food to maintain her formidable size. Perhaps one of the Wharf vendors had taken a liking to her and become her benefactor? Or perhaps she was simply a better hunter than a small, hobble-legged kitten.

Mari grew larger as she entered the lanky stage of kitten-hood, but the skin stretched tight over her bones. She took to following the brown tabby on her rounds, hoping to learn a few secrets. All she did was alienate the only cat that had hitherto deigned to tolerate her. After two days of letting Mari follow her around like a little white shadow, the brown tabby had had more than enough. She screamed profanities at Mari that made Flamond's language seem tame, and chased her, claws out, all the way to the very end of a slimy old wooden dock.

Mari cowered, but the brown tabby left a bright line of red blood on her nose as a reminder before leaving.

"Don't follow me," she meowled in a higher voice than Mari would have expected, trotting back down the dock. Then her caterwaul turned into a song of the night, joining with the yeowling voices of Flamond's gang in the distance. Mari listened in silence as the voices of the street diverged from song to screaming fights. Then they died away, entirely, and all that was left was the slapping sound of the waves.

THE WHITE FACE of the moon broke into strips of silver on the breaking wavelets of the bay. A gull cried, and Mari heard harbor seals barking to each other in the distance. She wished she could swim out to them. She would even brave water, if it would bring her to animals that wouldn't revile her like the Wharf cats. But she wasn't a seal. And the gulls, gathered on the top of an arch over the dock, wouldn't welcome her, even if she could sprout wings from her back and fly up to join them.

She'd give anything to get away from her life on the Wharf.

As Mari watched the waves, she noticed the tell-tale splashes of fish jumping in the water. Her life was suffused with the smell of fish, but their taste was expensive and rare. Catching mice was faster and more reliable than begging for scraps by purring at tourists. Besides, Mari hated to beg. She hated the tourists' transient pity.

Mari wondered if she could catch a fish. She would have to get closer to the water, so Mari followed the dock back inland. There was a metal grate fence to keep the tourists away from the water, but Mari was still small enough to squeeze under it. On the other side, large shadowy rocks lined the land, leading down to the water. Mari clambered over and down them until she set her paws on a flat-topped rock close enough to the surface of the water that lapping wavelets left it wet on top.

The dampness under her paw pads made Mari shiver, and a sudden gust of wind over the bay ruffled her white fur. If she meant to catch a fish, she would have to be patient. And ready. If ever a fish jumped close enough for her short paw to reach it, she would have only an instant to react. Mari crouched, muscles tensed, and prepared herself for a long dull night, hopefully to be followed by one bright moment of adrenaline.

Cats don't dream when they nap, but the world turns hazy seen through slit shut eyes.

The water began to glow. At first Mari thought she'd drifted into a doze, waiting to see a splash. Then a ringing started in her ears to match the silvery cast of the bay water. The ringing grew deep and rich. Mari twisted her ears, skewing them side to side, but she couldn't figure out the ringing's source. Then the ringing was broken by the sound of splashing, and a flash of light blinded Mari.

White ears flattened, and golden eyes blinked. When Mari's eyes opened again, there was a vision before her.

A human might have noticed the graceful curve of the mermaid's waist as her porcelain skin gave way to silver scales, or the stunning set of her emerald eyes. But Mari saw only the tip of her tail. The mermaid's body disappeared beneath the glassy surface of the water and reappeared where the very tip of her tail broke the surface. That tiny net of silver fin twitched just enough to create circles of concentric ripples.

Mari pounced.

After an embarrassment of water and horrible wetness, thrashing and coughing, Mari found herself lifted by careful hands. She slashed a paw clawfully to protect herself, but the hands squeezed her middle—a pressure halfway between comfort and warning. Mari staid her claws.

"Silly kitten," the mermaid said.

"Silly fish!" Mari countered.

The mermaid's soft laughter let Mari know her mewing had been understood. It also rankled her pride. Dismissive amusement was barely better than pity. The water in Mari's fur didn't help with her pride, and, as soon as the mermaid set her down on a rock, Mari set to work cleaning her wet fur with her little cat's tongue.

As she bathed, Mari sneaked glances at the mermaid, lounging in the shallow water beside the rocky shore. Her hair was long and silver, though her face was young. It fell over her shoulders and tumbled down to the water, moving with the slightest tilt of the mermaid's head. The movement captivated Mari, though she tried not to give her feelings away by staring at it.

When her bath was done, Mari's fur was still damp, but at least it was smoothed and clean. She sat herself neatly on her haunches and looked the mermaid in her eye. She was ready to speak with this vision, fully in command of her own dignity again. Then the mermaid turned her head to look back out to sea, and a strand of her flaxen hair whipped along the rock in front of Mari.

Mari pounced and found herself playing with the silken strands like an uncouth kitten. All dignity gone. Laughter reached her ears, but she couldn't care. Her paws and claws were too busy scrabbling at the surface of the rock, trying vainly to capture the living strands.

"Hey fish-bringer," said a familiar high-pitched meow.

Mari looked up, eyes wide, to see the brown tabby on the far side of the metal fence. Remembering the sting on her nose from earlier, Mari darted between two of the rocks, disappearing in the chasm between.

A quick jump hoisted the tabby's girth to the top of the fence and over. Looking out from her hiding place, Mari could see something gleam in the brown tabby's mouth as she awkwardly scrambled down the rocks. The tabby placed her rectangular burden on the ground, before speaking to the mermaid again. "I brought your bitter milk bar. Where's my fish?" the tabby spat.

Mari's golden eyes followed the tabby's gaze to the mermaid's face.

Emerald eyes narrowed, and the mermaid said, "You can be more polite than that, Buttercup."

The tip of Mari's tail twitched in mirth at learning her fellow stray's name, but she knew better than to reveal herself with any sound. She didn't need any more scratches today.

The brown tabby—Buttercup—flattened her ears and

lowered her eyes. Then she meowed in even tones, "Lady Elayne of the Mer-Country, may I please have my fish?"

A smile graced the mermaid's lips like warm rain on a summer day. She reached toward Buttercup as if to pet her. Mari felt her back arch up as if to meet a phantom mirror of the mermaid's hand, but the striped brown girth of Buttercup's back arched downward. Her furry brown belly brushed the ground, and the mermaid's hand stopped short. Sadness touched the mermaid's smile, but her slender fingers drew back. She reached for the rectangular offering instead—a foil wrapped bar of the darkest chocolate.

Mari recognized the scent from her early days, living with her littermates in a warm cardboard box. The man who owned her then liked chocolate, but the scent of this chocolate was much stronger, darker, richer. His chocolate had been weak and sugary in comparison.

The mermaid examined the bar, tracing her fingertips along the ornate script that read *Ghirardelli*. Her eyes rose from the bar and stared into the broken darkness of the night. The garish lights of the San Francisco skyline stretched out on the hill, glittering above them. "I wish I could go to the magical place where they make these," she said.

Buttercup hissed. "It's horrible."

"Describe it to me," the mermaid pressed.

Buttercup's ears flattened, and her whiskers turned down. Mari recognized the look from shortly before Buttercup scratched her.

"Do you want *descriptions*," Buttercup meowed, "or bitter milk in trade for your fish?"

The sadness on the mermaid's lips was replaced with resignation. "You're a cantankerous old cat," she said, but she reached under the water and pulled out a string.

Dangling from the end was a wriggling, gleaming fish. It's scales were dull gray compared to the mermaid's gleaming silver, but it looked delectable to Mari nonetheless.

Mari flexed her claws and licked her chops. It took all the restraint she had to keep from pouncing out of her hiding place. She wanted to feel her claws in the flesh of that fish, but she didn't want to feel Buttercup's claws in her face.

Mari watched Buttercup bat the tempting treat senseless and then crouch over its corpse, devouring every last morsel of its sweet smelling flesh. Mari hoped that Buttercup would finish and leave the bones, leave the shore, leave the mermaid for Mari to talk to again. Perhaps the Lady Elayne would reach to pet her as she had reached toward Buttercup...

But Buttercup crouched over the remains of the fish, licking her chops and chewing on bones, long after the mermaid took her bar of chocolate and left. Her final act before sinking under the surface of the water was to draw a gnarled, twisted piece of twig from a belt of seaweed at her waist, and bestow a shimmering gleam of light on the oblivious, feasting tabby.

Mari stayed hidden, shivering between the rocks, marveling at what she'd seen and wishing she were Buttercup.

OVER THE NEXT FEW DAYS, Mari came to one definite decision: she must make her own deal with the mermaid Elayne. Thus, she must learn how to steal chocolate like Buttercup to offer in trade. However, trailing Buttercup had not worked out well for Mari, so she needed to locate the chocolate herself. Fortunately, that part was easy. Her nose led her to it. Up the hill from the Wharf was a shop that absolutely reeked of the bitter brown substance. The hard part would be breaking in and acquiring it.

Surely, Mari reasoned, Buttercup must have secret strategies for making it past the glass walls, through the crowds of feet, and into the chocolate soaked air of the shop. Mari's spiteful side told her to blackmail Buttercup with the frou-frou, flowery truth of her name. It must be worth *something* to Buttercup to keep that truth from Flamond and his gang. But, when it came down to it, Mari was too afraid.

Instead, she lurked outside the shop, peering through the windows. She watched the humans sit at their tables, spooning fluffy whipped cream and melting, dripping ice cream out of metal bowls filled to heaping with scoops of the colorful confection. She licked her chops, dreaming of the creamy taste, but when the craving for it cramped her stomach, Mari had to give up her vigil and hunt plain street mice for her supper.

At night, Mari returned to the rocky edge of the bay where she'd met the mermaid, and stared out over the black, star-studded water, hoping to see that glowing vision again. Not that she'd have anything to trade her for the gift of a succulent fish... Mari would have to try harder.

The next day, Mari haunted the sidewalk in front of Ghirardelli Square, miaowing prettily at the shop's customers. She purred and pranced, smiling at them hopefully, but they spared her only patronizing scritches and pats. No bars of chocolate. No invitations to join the humans at the tables inside. She would have to slip in, uninvited.

Mari waited for the right group to open the door. Groups with small children were too erratic, and Mari was sure she'd end up stepped upon. So, she waited for a group of gangly college students. Mari timed her dash through the glassed door carefully, scampering through as quickly as she could with her gimp leg, hidden among the sneakered-feet of the college students.

Once inside, Mari slunk close to the wall, fast-walking so that she looked like she had at least eight legs. She daren't run outright without knowing where she was heading. The tables, on their central poles with forests of chair legs around them, offered little concealment.

Feet were everywhere! Mari's claws slipped on the tiled floor as she scrabbled to keep out from under the hard soles of all the shoes. An island counter with shelves under it, lined with shiny bags, cellophane-wrapped boxes, and jars of chocolate, seemed like a temporary refuge—but too many eyes were on the chocolate; too many hands reaching for it. And the jars, bags, and boxes themselves were too large for Mari to steal and carry off in her small mouth.

The noise and bustle of all of the crowding humans already had Mari's head spinning when she suddenly found herself face to face with the glaring, frowning, hissing visage of Buttercup. Her brown ears were flat; her angry eyes narrowed; and her paw was drawn back to strike, claws bared.

A strangled squeak escaped Mari's throat. She turned tail and ran, haphazardly scrabbling into ankles and catching her claws in shoelaces on the way. She didn't stop when she got outside. She fled, limping, all the way down the hill to the Wharf, her sad and lonely home. But her home, no less.

Mari watched the bay that night, disconsolate. Her hopes of stealing chocolate had been dashed, and her hopes of running into the mermaid again were fading. As the moon sank into the waters of the bay, Mari felt her heart sink as well.

She could hardly believe her eyes when the water before her began to shimmer and glow. Her last comfort had been to believe that her failure in the chocolate shop didn't really matter. The Lady Elayne was a vision—unreal or, at least, unrepeatable. But now she was faced with the sight of the lovely lady rising from the water.

Mari's whiskers drooped. Buttercup would surely be here soon to slash the nose of any young cat in the way. And Mari had nothing to offer the mermaid, but she felt herself drawn past the metal fence and down to the wet rocks at the water's level anyway.

"I tried to steal chocolate for you," Mari mewed. Her eyes traced the cascading flow of the mermaid's silver locks. Her head tilted in fascination, ears askew, but she restrained herself from pouncing this time.

"Brave kitten," Elayne answered.

"As brave as Buttercup!" Mari blustered. Though, she remembered turning tail to run, and her ears dipped. "I couldn't figure out how Buttercup does it," she admitted. "I spent days studying the shop." Mournfully, Mari told Elayne everything she had seen. The chocolate shop was a fortress, designed to keep out stray cats, admitting only humans.

As Mari told her story, however, wrought with details of the chocolate shop's layout and design, Elayne's eyes began to shine. She clasped her hands and sighed.

"Thank you, kitten," she said, when Mari's story of woe was through. "I have wished for ages that I could go to that chocolate shop, but I don't have magic strong enough to let me walk on land." She took the gnarled old twig that was holstered to the belt of braided seaweed tied about her waist and held it out, pointing toward Mari. "Buttercup brings me chocolate, but she won't bring me tales. If I give you the same glamour that I've given Buttercup, will you brave the chocolate shop again? And bring me more stories?"

"Glamour?" Mari mewed, crouching low at the thought of Buttercup. Surely that big, brown tabby would be here soon to make her trade with Elayne. Mari didn't care to run into her again, nor to spend the whole night hiding behind a rock.

Elayne raised the gnarled old twig to her forehead. With a flick of her wrist, there was a flash of light.

Then Mari narrowed her eyes at the strange sight she saw: instead of a mermaid, reclining in the water, there was a silver kitten, much like herself, treading her paws to stay afloat. The kitten laughed with Elayne's musical voice. Then Mari blinked at the sight of the mermaid's body, superimposed like a reflection on a window, over the kitten. The illusion ended, and the Lady Elayne was herself again: a beautiful, silver-tailed and silver-haired mermaid. Mari felt dizzy.

"That's how Buttercup steals the chocolate for me," Elayne said, "without anyone stepping on her tail or rushing her off with a broom. I give her a glamour."

Mari's gold eyes were wide. "The people see her as... another one of them?"

Elayne smiled and lowered the twig toward Mari. "Will you go back to the shop and explore it for me?"

Mari forgot her pride: "Every nook and cranny!" she exclaimed, lifting herself to her haunches to bring her nose closer to the magical end of Elayne's gnarled twig. Her whiskers felt a vibration in the air near it.

Elayne flicked the twig again. There was another flash of light, but Mari didn't feel any different. She poked her head over the surface of the water, hoping to catch sight of the glamour in the glimmer of the water's reflection.

She saw only a small white cat with a skeptical look in her yellow eyes.

Then she heard the sound of Buttercup meowling in the distance. Mari could stay no longer. She scurried off before Elayne could tell her when to come again. Or give her the fish she'd earned by telling stories of Ghirardelli Square.

IN THE HARSH light of day, Mari began to wonder if it wasn't all a dream—the mermaid, the magic wand, the glamour, and the promise of fish. Sometimes when she was hungry, she could see mice dance before her. They taunted her with waltzes and jigs, but when she swatted them, her claws touched only air. Hunger visions.

The Lady Elayne was a much more detailed and elaborate vision, but, surely, she was also a vision?

Mari decided to put the mermaid and her promises out of her mind and go about her normal life. As the day progressed, however, Mari noticed strange things happening. People walking toward her stepped to the side instead of treading relentlessly on, unaware of the kitten who must scurry out of the way or be trod upon. This change was subtle, and Mari wondered if she was imagining it until a person—a tourist with a camera in his hand—walked right up to her, knelt down, and held the camera forward.

"Would you take our picture?" the tourist asked, gesturing back at his family.

Mari twisted her ears around and glanced from side to side, looking and listening for who the tourist could mean.

He smiled encouragingly and waggled a shiny silver

rectangle at her enticingly. It was almost enough to convince Mari she should take it... but she had no hands. This tourist was mad.

As Mari stared at the madman with flattened ears, another tourist came by and offered to take the desired picture. Mari was freed of the ministrations of the madman but not the mystery that caused his behavior.

Everywhere she went, Mari found this strangeness in people's behavior toward her. They were deferential, respectful, *aware of her*, without condescension or pity. Mari wasn't sure what to make of this change. But she liked it.

A few times Mari experimented with mewing at people, but she invariably received confusion in response. *"I'm sorry, what was that?"* *"Say that again, I couldn't quite make out what you said?"* Always coupled with contorted, displeased faces.

Whatever magic the mermaid's glamour had clothed Mari with, clearly, did not extend to her voice.

With a renewed faith in her nighttime visions, Mari set out to complete the task Lady Elayne had set her. She limped up the hill, back to the chocolate shop in Ghirardelli Square. This time, though, she walked right up to the front door. And, as she passed the large windows, she could see herself reflected in their glass—except, her reflection was strange to her.

A scrawny human girl dressed in plain clothes with short blonde hair and startling yellow eyes stared back at Mari from the murky mirror world of reflections. That was what the humans saw. Mari felt a surge of empowerment seeing the magical avatar that Lady Elayne had created for her. In that form, Mari was an equal with all the people of the Wharf. In that form, Mari was able to walk right into Ghirardelli Square.

Except, she had to wait for a real human to open the

door. And, once she was inside, she couldn't speak to the workers wielding their ice cream scoops behind the counter to order a milky, creamy sundae. Nor could she pay for one, even if she could have ordered it.

Mari sighed. The reflection in the window may have shown a human girl, and the real humans might see one—but she was only a hungry kitten.

Mari was still deciding how to proceed when she saw Buttercup, tail high, strolling past the windows toward the entrance of the shop. The mist-like shape of a heavy-set, bob-haired brunette woman clung to Buttercup like the smell of too much perfume. Mari could hardly believe she hadn't seen the effect of Elayne's glamour on Buttercup before.

Not wishing to encounter her foul-tempered friend, Mari scurried toward the back of the shop, hoping to stay out of sight. On the other side of all the tables, occupied by happy humans eating ice cream, there was a low wall partitioning the shop. Taking a calculated risk, Mari poised herself, wiggling her tail, and leapt up, up, over the wall.

On the far side, she found herself staring at great vats with giant wheels pouring, stirring, mixing an endless current of milky, liquid chocolate in their machinery. Mari stared transfixed, forgetting that her glamour was not nearly as well hidden as her own small kitten's body.

Buttercup passed by without seeing her young rival for Lady Elayne's affections. A young man working the ice cream counter, however, saw Mari's glamour—seemingly a grade school girl, standing in a part of the store where she didn't belong.

"Hey, you!" he said, leaving his post at the counter behind. The other ice cream scoopers took over his role seamlessly, allowing him the freedom to pursue confronting

Mari. "What are you doing back here?" He looked around the shop; "Where are your parents?"

Mari stared at the shop boy with wide golden eyes. She miewed an answer, but he couldn't understand her.

"Look," he said, scratching his head beneath the crisp white hat he wore as part of his uniform. "You can't be back here. We need to find your parents."

Mari miewed again, and the shop boy frowned. He couldn't have explained it, but there was an endearing, pitiful quality to the girl he saw. Mari's kitten-nature shone through the glamour, pulling at his heartstrings, and compelling the shop boy to help her.

"Just come with me," he said. "I'll fix you some ice cream, and you can eat it while I look for your parents."

Mari felt a glow inside that threatened to overflow her small body in purrs.

The shop boy fixed a simple bowl of vanilla ice cream for the little lost girl and set her up at a table close to the front counter where he could keep an eye on her. For Mari's part, she jumped right up on the table next to the bowl of ice cream, hoping her glamour body would continue to sit nicely on the chair. The magic obliged.

The shop boy set to work, speaking to his supervisor and then checking the rest of the shop for anyone missing a little girl. Meanwhile, Mari set to work eating the first ice cream she'd ever tasted. It was sweet and cold. Smooth and creamy. The intensity of the experience nearly overwhelmed her.

After licking the last smears of melted ice cream from an almost clean bowl, Mari brought a paw to her face and began washing her sticky whiskers. Then she saw Buttercup: her nemesis in this game of mermaid glamours was still in the shop, standing in a line of waiting humans. At the end of the line stood one of the shop workers, holding a silver platter and handing out samples. When Buttercup reached the front of the line, the shop worker knelt down and held the platter toward her. Buttercup's glamour reached out with a hand to grab a chocolate square; Buttercup herself took it in her teeth. She trotted out of the shop, a shiny foil wrapped square dangling from her mouth.

Aha! That was how Buttercup got her chocolate.

Mari jumped down from her table, leaving the empty ice cream bowl behind. She trotted toward the man with the samples, tail held high. Unfortunately, her own shop boy intervened. She tried to get past him, but he knelt down, holding his arms out, and blocked her. He explained to her that they couldn't find her parents. He seemed confused and frustrated. Mostly, he wanted Mari to stay put until a guardian for her could be found.

But none would be found. Although Mari had wandered through the Wharf all morning, no one had troubled themselves with whether she was alone. Not until she broke a rule—jumping behind that wall, standing too close to the machines mixing chocolate.

Mari felt frustrated by her kitten's tongue. She couldn't explain herself. She couldn't behave the way the shop boy expected. His demeanor and rising concern was drawing more and more attention. Mari wasn't sure how this would play out, but she decided it was time to run. So, she made a dash, as quickly as she could, for the front door.

The shop boy cried out, and customers jumped aside startled as a young girl seemingly ran right through them, ghostlike and insubstantial. In reality, it was only a small white kitten, darting deftly between their feet.

Mari disappeared into the crowd of tourists. Agitated, she wandered among them, wondering whether any more humans would confront her. At first, it had felt empowering for the people to treat her like one of them. But she was not one of them. And it turned out that it made her feel even more lonely and isolated to be misunderstood than to be ignored.

Mari missed being anonymous, too small to notice at the people's feet, and she hoped the glamour would wear off soon.

THE SIGHT of an unaccompanied young girl drew more and more attention as the day darkened, waning into evening. So, Mari gave up on mousing, after hours of fruitlessly dodging workers on the Wharf who scared away her quarry with unhelpful questions: *"Hey, little girl, are you lost?"* *"Where are you going?"* *"Where are your parents?"* Everyone was against her.

Mari ducked behind one of the seafood restaurants and ensconced herself behind a foul smelling brown dumpster. No one could see her—or her glamour—there. No one bothered her while she waited for the fullness of night.

Shaky with hunger, Mari came out from her hiding place well after midnight. The bowl of ice cream she'd eaten earlier in the afternoon, while delicious, was not sustaining. In fact, the richness of the milk had long since turned into a twisted, aching knot in her belly.

Before she could focus on the concerns of her stomach, however, Mari needed to know if the Lady Elayne was there. She was filled with a confusion of emotions that told her to scold the mermaid for betraying her with this glamour that kept her from mousing—but, also, she hoped, deep in her heart, that the Lady Elayne would be pleased with her.

She wanted to share the story of that glorious bowl of ice

cream, reliving it in the retelling, and she hoped—so secretly that she hardly admitted the hope even to herself—that Elayne would reach out to stroke her, as she had once reached out to pet Buttercup. Mari would not shrink away.

Quick-footed as she could, Mari lopsidedly ran to the rocky edge of the bay. To her surprise, Elayne was already reclined in the water, this time under the wooden walkway of the pier, brushing out her long silver tresses.

Mari crouched at the fence and stared through the metal grating. She watched, mesmerized, while the mermaid divided her hair into strands, separated by her nimble fingers. Deftly, Elayne wove the strands into a long braid, then another, and another. Then she wove the braids together, and coiled them over her head, pinning them in place like a crown. Only curling tendrils were left unbound to frame her face.

Mari found herself purring. Something about the quick, snaking motion of the strands of hair stirred a feeling of excitement deep inside Mari. It made her heart beat fast like hunting. It reminded her of being a tiny kitten, safe and warm, surrounded by love, and playing with a dangled string.

Before Mari could present herself to the mermaid, she heard the ominous sound of growling come from behind.

The sound grew and multiplied. Twisting her ears about, Mari could hear it from several directions. She crouched low, flattening her body as close to the ground as she could. Then she crawled forward, under the metal fence, and crammed herself into a crevasse between several of the large rocks lining the bay's edge. With her ears flattened, Mari could still hear the growling; peering out from between the rocks, she could see several of Flamond's gang strutting across the pavement, tails swishing wildly.

Preceding them, with a frantic, haggard look, Buttercup spat and cursed around the shining square of foil, hanging from her teeth.

"Hey, Dirt-Stripes!" one of the gang yowled.

Another called out, "Whattaya got there, Fat Cat?"

Melting out of the shadows as if he were made of them, Flamond appeared among his followers. "Yeah, Plumpy-Puss," he said, with a snide hiss, "that don't look like yours. It looks like *mine*." His tail curled at the tip, showing how safe and confident he felt.

Buttercup's tail was a brush of fright. "This is mine," she hissed. "I caught it." She dropped the square of foil on the ground and crouched over it, like a mamma bird protecting her egg.

Buttercup hissed and snarled for all she was worth, but when two of Flamond's gang—both fit, young cats, sporting the strong, developed upper bodies of unneutered, feral males—got within striking range, she scrabbled back and away.

The square of foil lay unprotected on the concrete, gleaming bright with reflected light from a nearby street-lamp. Flamond snickered. His guards backed respectfully out of his way as he came to examine his prize.

Flamond stared at the square of foil. He touched his nose to it. Gingerly, he batted it with a paw. Then he tested it with his teeth. His ears skewed in confusion. "This is your secret?" he hissed. He tried chewing on it again, but the distaste on his face was clear.

"Don't ruin it," Buttercup miewed pitifully.

"Why not?" Flamond asked. "It's mine now. What do you do with it, anyway? It don't taste very good." He kept gnawing on the foil anyway. Probably out of simple spite.

One of Flamond's guards meowled, "If she don't tell ya, Boss, can we scratch 'er?"

"Yah, let's kick 'er eyes out," yowled the other one.

Mari could see Buttercup's demeanor sagging.

Mari might not have been treated well by the fat, brown tabby, but they had spent many afternoons in the sun together. And they shared the secret bond of Lady Elayne. And Mari admired Buttercup for protecting that secret, in spite of the growing threats from Flamond's gang. No one deserved to be bullied by them.

With her heart beating a mile a minute, Mari crawled out of her hidden crevasse, back under the fence, and up to Buttercup. She crept past the brown tabby's girth, daring to let the side of her body brush up against Buttercup's. Her fur felt smooth next to the fluffed bristle of Buttercup's coat.

For a single moment, Mari locked eyes with Buttercup. She could see sorrow and terror there. Then Mari turned to Flamond, and meowed as bravely as she could, "It's for me. She brings them for me."

The heckling voices of Flamond's gang quieted down, and Flamond himself narrowed his eyes at Mari. His voice cold, he asked, "And, what, pray tell, do you want with them?"

Mari's mind raced. She knew Flamond was afraid of her malformed leg, so she stepped forward with an exaggerated limp and false bravado. "I eat them," she said.

Flamond's ears flattened at the nearness of the gimp kitten. In a hiss, he asked, "*Why.*"

Trying to quell her own fear and exacerbate Flamond's, Mari said, "They feed the demon living in my leg." She hopped a little, as if she couldn't keep balance with her gimp leg. "If I don't eat them, the demon will eat the rest of me."

Flamond stayed crouched over his foil prize, superstition battling with reason inside him.

"And once it eats me," Mari said, pressing on, "it'll need a new cat to eat." Although it made her heart trip to do it, Mari forced herself to step closer to the powerful black cat. He could strike her down with one paw. She had no doubt he could kill her in less than a minute. But, she terrified him with her invented demon.

Flamond's tail began to bush out. Trying to hide his fear from his followers, Flamond spat the foil square out and batted it with a paw, sending it skidding across the concrete towards Mari. "Keep your demon food," he hissed. He turned to his guards, "Come on. Let's leave Dirt-Stripes here to mamma-ing her broken kitten. She's not worth our time."

Flamond turned tail and stalked away with only a line of fur along his spine fluffed up. His two guards hesitated a moment, but then they followed suit. They cackled at Buttercup, taunting her as they left. The rest of the gang echoed the guards' laughter, but one by one they shrank into the shadows, disappearing as well.

MARI AND BUTTERCUP crouched on the pavement, alone in the darkness. As her heart slowed, Mari dared to step forward and pick up the foil square with her teeth. It swayed, hanging from her mouth, as she brought it over to drop beside Buttercup.

The brown tabby made no move toward her prize.

"Don't you want it?" Mari asked, pawing at the foil square. "To give to Elayne?"

Buttercup's ears were still flat, and her eyes wide and

stricken as she looked up at Mari. "You're not taking it?" Buttercup meowled.

Mari remembered the feel of Buttercup's claws across her nose. It seemed like she should feel triumphant now that Buttercup was deferring to her, but she only felt uncomfortable. "It's yours," she miewed. "I have my own gift to bring the Lady."

Buttercup scoffed. She'd recovered from her fright quickly, but she didn't entirely return to her usual chilly demeanor toward Mari. "Thank you," she meowed. Then she picked up the foil square, wiggled her tail, and leapt straight into the air. Her feet barely touched the top of the metal fence on her way over it.

Mari followed after her, squeezing beneath the fence. As she clambered down the rocks, she saw Buttercup ahead of her.

Buttercup dropped the square of foil on a rock at the edge of the water and meowed to the Lady Elayne, "This bitter milk was unusually hard to come by. I think it's worth *two* fish."

The Lady Elayne laughed and said, "Fine, I'll bring you another fish tomorrow, and you don't have to trade me anything for it."

Buttercup meowed, "I think you have two fish on you tonight."

"I might," the Lady said. "But one of them is promised to another."

Buttercup grumbled, but she took the single, wriggling fish held out toward her anyway. Gleefully, she batted it senseless, playing and murdering simultaneously. When she finally settled down to the important work of eating, the Lady Elayne reached out and stroked Buttercup's brown fur.

Buttercup's body flattened, but she was too busy with the fish to entirely escape.

Mari watched with jealousy in her heart. Then the Lady Elayne turned toward her, and the jealousy inside twisted around, turning into a glowing warmth. She rushed to the edge of the water and began telling the mermaid all about her day in words so fast they ran together into a drawn out caterwaul.

"Slow down, Little Cat," Elayne said. "How can I savor the story you've brought me when you tell it so fast?"

Buttercup looked up from her eviscerated fish, and said through bloodied whiskers, "The humans gave you a bowl of *ice cream?* I've clearly been doing this all wrong."

The Lady Elayne chuckled and reached to scratch the fat tabby's ears, but Buttercup shrugged away from her hand. So, instead, Elayne held her long, slender fingers out toward Mari.

The white kitten raised her head, pressing it into the mermaid's hand. Smooth fingernails scratched deeply against the base of her ear. So satisfying. Purrs rose from Mari's body, pulled out by the rhythmic scritching.

Tourists might scritch Mari's ears if she danced and meowled for them, but it didn't mean anything. They didn't know her, and she would never see them again. If she told stories of ice cream to the Lady Elayne, maybe she would keep coming back. Maybe she would keep scratching her ears, every night, if the stories Mari told her were good enough.

Mari pressed her head so hard against Elayne's hand that her whole kitten's body toppled over, rolling her into a melted mess of purrs. Her paws curled in the air above her, and her eyes closed in contentment.

Buttercup snorted at Mari's display of indignity, but Mari

didn't care anymore. When the scritching ended, Elayne dangled the second silvery gleam of fish above Mari who batted it delightedly with all four paws. Finally, she grasped it tightly with her front claws, and she kicked it soundly to death with her feet before rolling off of her back to begin eating it.

The fish's smell was pungent, but the taste was sweet. It had a much deeper more complicated flavor than the ice cream. It tasted cool and oily, salty like the ocean air, and delicately flaky against her teeth. It was everything she'd dreamed it would be.

Once Mari's belly was full, she felt much better. She hadn't realized how badly the hunger had been gnawing at her stomach until it was gone.

"Now, Little Cat, can you tell me about the ice cream more slowly?" Elayne said.

Mari settled comfortably on her paws, wrapping her tail around her loaf-like body, and began retelling her tale. She was brave and clever in her story. The ice cream was guarded by towering walls, dangerous mechanical vats, and sphinx-like shop boys who assaulted her with their riddling questions. Yet, through it all, she prevailed, tricking the humans into setting a feast before her, and serving her like a queen.

Buttercup chuckled. "If that's how you describe the ice cream shop, I'd love to hear how you describe me." Buttercup had finished eating her fish as well, but she hadn't left, instead being drawn in by the story. "Were you attacked by a gigantic brown bear, wandering lost through the streets of San Francisco?"

Mari glared at Buttercup. "Yes," she said. "But then the bear was attacked by a pack of wolves, and I had to rescue her."

Buttercup twitched her tail tip, but there was a smile in her eyes. She liked seeing herself as a bear.

At the sound of movement in the water, both cats looked back towards their mermaid. The Lady Elayne had shifted herself, sinking deeper into the water, until it came midway up her shoulders. "I have to go soon," she said. "But thank you for the stories. And the chocolate. Do you want another glamour, so you can do it again?"

Mari crept to the edge of the rocks and peered into the water. She didn't see the reflection of the young human girl, and she felt relieved. "No," she said, reluctantly. She feared she was giving up fish and ice cream and love, but she couldn't stand the idea of that hideous ghostly glamour clinging to her again. "I don't like pretending to be something I'm not."

"I do," Buttercup meowed. "I'm getting a bowl of ice cream tomorrow. I need to try that stuff for myself." As an afterthought, she added, "And I can tell you about it. I guess."

"See if you can get a different flavor?" Elayne asked, lifting her twig-like wand out of the water to touch the delicately striped fur on Buttercup's forehead. The air shifted around Buttercup, and Mari could see the ghostly shape of her human glamour reflected on the water.

"Now, I have to go," Elayne said.

Mari meowed, with all the fervency of youth, "I wish I could come with you."

The Lady Elayne hesitated. She'd already sunk so low in the water that the surface lapped against the bottom of her chin. She stared at Mari with a puzzled expression, and, rising a little out of the water, said, "Do you mean that?"

Mari remembered belonging to the man who had dangled string for her and made her a cozy nest in a cardboard box. She had felt safe and loved then. Ever since, she'd wandered the streets of the Wharf feeling like an outcast, sent into exile. Sometimes, she saw cats sitting behind the windows of buildings that were closed to her. Those cats looked safe and happy, like she remembered feeling.

The water that Elayne threatened to sink behind felt like another pane of glass, separating her from a home where she could feel safe and belong.

"Oh so much," Mari sighed with a purr. "I wish I could go with you, down into the ocean, and be your swimming cat, and you could be my mermaid."

The Lady Elayne placed her hands on the rock beside Mari and drew herself higher out of the water. She looked down at the little cat, narrowing her eyes in thought. The white kitten before her smiled with golden eyes and purred with her entire body.

"I can grant that wish for you, Mari," Elayne said. "I don't have enough magic to change my own body into one that can walk on land, but I have enough to change your small body into one that can swim down to live in the Mer-Country with me. And I would like to have a swimming cat."

Buttercup scoffed and hissed, verily sputtering in horror at the idea of so much water. "You'd be wet all the time!"

Mari assured Elayne that she wouldn't mind, and the mermaid drew out her wand again.

The changes started at Mari's nose. Her nostrils narrowed, growing the muscles necessary to let them close against water. Then her ears grew smaller and rounder, developing valves inside to protect them against water too. Her fur thickened, and webbing grew between her toes. Her tail broadened like a rudder, and her spine grew longer. Other changes happened deep inside, invisibly altering her body chemistry to let her breathe like a mermaid, both from air and water in turn.

Mari sat back on her haunches and held her newly webbed paws in front of her. She twisted her ears, but they didn't move as freely. Her spine, however, now let her twist all the way around and see her broadened tail.

For all the world, she looked like a little albino otter, except for her golden eyes which hadn't changed.

Mari dove into the water of the bay, and took her first strokes as a swimming cat. She played in the water, delighting in the new sensation. Mari's left back leg was still malformed, but she found it didn't matter as much while swimming.

Buttercup scowled, backing away from the edge of the water to avoid getting splashed. "I'll be back tomorrow," she meowled. "With more stories of ice cream."

"So will we," the mermaid said, looking at her new swimming cat. "And I think Mari will have stories for you of chasing fishes under the ocean."

10

MAGTWILLA AND THE MOUSE

HEAVY WITH KITTENS, Magtwilla made a choice. She'd been a housecat before, and she'd spent time being feral. Although she disliked the restrictive interference of the clothed primates, she had to admit that their houses with reliable food and warmth would be the better environment for a litter of kittens. So, Magtwilla selected a nice house and set about the work of charming the clothed primate who lived there. In mere days, the primate took her in, strapped an offensively pink collar around her throat, and took to calling her Jenny. Todd was laughably easy to manipulate with a simple purr. Magtwilla felt she'd done well by her unborn kittens.

The litter of three was born in a cozy sock drawer. Warm, soft, and infinitely precious, the three tiny kittens gave meaning to a life that had previously been nothing more than a fight to survive.

The clothed primate called her darlings Socks, Boots, and Mittens. Magtwilla appreciated his enthusiasm for his role of provider for her and the kittens, but his idea of a good name was terrible. Magtwilla gave each of her kittens a proper feline name in the traditional ceremony held when a kitten first opens her eyes.

Twillatha was a gray tabby, just like the handsome tom who fathered her. Magtori was a calico girl like her mother. And Jenwilla was a solid gray who bonded almost instantly with the clothed primate. Magtwilla had to tolerate Todd holding her much more than she would have liked.

Nonetheless, those early weeks of her litter's kittenhood were the happiest of Magtwilla's life. Twillatha, Magtori, and Jenwilla filled their mother's heart with love and pride. Every day, she overflowed with purrs, watching her kittens stumble about, pouncing, playing, and learning the nature of their world. As the kittens grew steadier on their paws, Magtwilla began teaching them what they'd need to know to survive when they escaped from Todd's house.

Twillatha took to her mother's teachings the best. She wiggled her tabby haunches like a pro and could track a single dust mote, falling through a shaft of sunlight, only to pounce on it perfectly as it hit the floor. Magtwilla would never have to worry about Twillatha being able to feed herself. She would be a natural huntress.

Magtwilla didn't worry about Magtori either. While the baby Calico showed less interest in hunting, preferring to stay cuddled close to her mother, a true mama's little kitten, she was wise and cautious beyond her age. She listened closely with wide golden eyes—both to the lessons her mother told her and to the signs and tiny noises in the environment around her. Her ears constantly tracked the sounds of passing cars on the street outside Todd's house, and the sound of Todd's footsteps always sent Magtori darting to her mother's side.

Jenwilla, however, worried her mother greatly. It was as if she'd been born more domesticated than the others. She was too comfortable sleeping on cushions and eating dried pellets from ceramic bowls. She was too comfortable with Todd's ungainly primate hands on her. And when Todd brought a group of clothed primates to visit them all, Jenwilla showed a bizarre and unnatural interest in them.

Magtwilla didn't know why, but it gave her stomach butterflies to watch her cloud-gray baby skitter and play for the visiting primates, batting at string and purring loudly when they petted her. She wanted to call her daughter away from them, but her own fear of the visitors kept her back. So, when they left Todd's house, holding her daughter in their grabby primate hands, she was cowering in the corner, between the sofa and the wall. Magtori cuddled next to her. Twillatha was busy stalking a mouse that lived behind the refrigerator in the kitchen.

When the front door opened again, Todd returned without the other primates. And without Jenwilla.

Magtwilla cried out piteously, and she rushed to the front window, only to watch one of the primate's mechanical monsters pull out of the driveway and drive away. She sat in the window all night, spurning Todd's offers of tuna water. By the early hours of the morning, she felt haggard and hopeless. Unable to do anything to bring her Jenwilla back. She'd made a deal with the devil, and one of her three precious kittens was gone.

Magtwilla spent the whole next day bathing her remaining kittens, against their strenuous dissents. As the soothing rhythm of washing their warm, struggling bodies, dragging her rough tongue over the soft napes of their necks, brought Magtwilla back to herself, she began to form a plan.

It was time to escape. Whether her two kittens were ready for life outside or not, it was better than the risk she ran if they stayed. So, Magtwilla set about finding a way out of the house she'd adopted for her kittens' nativity.

Unfortunately, leaving Todd's domicile turned out to be much harder than working her way into it. The windows and doors were all kept tight shut, except when Todd walked through the front one. She'd tried darting through the front door, but he always blocked her deftly with his feet. She'd never known of another primate who was so fastidious about keeping a cat inside its house! There were vents in the floor, but they were much too heavy for her to remove and their grates too fine to reach more than a single paw through. She tried all the cupboard doors, but they only led to cupboards. And when she tried clawing up the carpet around the edges of the room, the floor underneath was hard and solid. No escape there.

Exhausted, Magtwilla vowed to explore behind the refrigerator after a decent night's rest. If the invading mouse had found a way in, there must also be a way out. Hopefully, it would prove to be cat-sized. Not merely mouse-sized.

The next day, though, was not soon enough. For Todd brought more clothed primates to visit them, including more of the boisterous short ones who moved in startling, jerky ways. Magtwilla spat at them, and Magtori followed suit. But one of the shortest primates dragged a piece of ribbon over the floor in a halting, stop-start fashion that completely charmed Twillatha. The tabby baby's hunting instincts took over, and she pranced entrancingly for the primates.

Magtwilla watched her second daughter's goodbye dance in horror, presciently guessing what was coming this time. She steeled herself to attack the visiting primates, but Todd chased her and Magtori off before her claws found a solid, fleshly purchase. She heard them leave with Twillatha while she was still recovering in the next room.

She didn't wait in the window this time. Her first daughter had been gone for days. She knew that her second one wouldn't return either.

After many dark hours, while Magtori's soft purring and beseeching gold eyes couldn't console her, Magtwilla resolved that she would escape Todd's prison of a home and find her daughters. Wherever the evil primates who took them had gone, Twillatha and Jenwilla must be findable. She was a good hunter. She would track the mechanical monsters that had borne her kittens away, and they would all be reunited. They would live a wholesome, righteous life in the wild, far from the primates who tempted with easy food and damnable cages.

Magtwilla told Magtori her plan. Perhaps the kitten was too young to understand. Perhaps she was too used to the cushy life the devilish primates offered. Perhaps she was simply frightened by her mother's frantic demeanor and bored by a long morning of searching for a seemingly non-existent mouse hole behind the refrigerator. Truth be told, Magtori wasn't even sure that the mythical creatures that her mother called 'mice,' and her missing sister pretended to stalk, even existed.

She did know that the old lady who Todd brought to visit her smelled pleasantly of milk and fresh bread. This older primate moved slowly and steadily, unlike the younger ones, and Magtori was drawn to her long white hair. The silvery strands escaped from a waist-length braid in a way that intrigued Magtori. She felt drawn to approach the older lady and touch that braid, gently, with a claw-sheathed paw. It was love at first sight, between Magtori the shy baby Calico and this woman who'd come to visit her. As pure a love as ever forms between cat and human.

Magtwilla watched it happen, helpless to affect it. She sat on the floor, in the middle of the room, too numb to hide. She'd brought her kittens to this house to protect them. She'd chosen to raise them in a place where they'd be safe and warm, and she had kept their bodies safe. Yet, the insidious nature of the primates had wormed its way into her kittens' hearts and minds. She had lost them as surely now as if all three had died in the cold.

Todd returned from walking the demon-shaped-like-a-harmless-old-woman out with Magtori, and he scritched Magtwilla behind the ear.

"It's just us now," he said. "You're a good kitty, Jenny, and you don't want those tiresome kittens wearing you out."

Magtwilla miaowed, a hollow sound, filled with sadness. The human who had entrapped her didn't understand its meaning, but the mouse who lived behind the refrigerator was watching. And he did.

As the hours progressed to days, the mouse watched Magtwilla begin to waste away. She sat in the window dreaming of her kittens. She wouldn't touch the food Todd brought her. The mouse feared Magtwilla, but his stomach was empty and a poorly-healed broken paw kept him from returning outdoors. The more food he'd stolen, the more careful Todd had become with his pantry. Now all the food was locked up tight, except for the bowl of milk and fish that perennially sat before the fading cat who disdained it.

Tiny brown eyes cautiously watched wide golden ones as the mouse began to dare approaching his natural predator. With each step, his heart beat faster, and his paws quivered worse. When the gold eyes finally turned and saw him, the mouse froze. But Magtwilla did not attack. She didn't raise a paw to strike him, and his hunger slowly conquered his fear. The small brown body crept up to Magtwilla's bowl. He placed his paws on the edge, and he stared into eyes that had spent days searching for something they would never find.

The brown mouse was nothing like her kittens, and, yet, he was small and soft and warm. "Are you a kitten?" she miaowed.

The mouse shook all over, but it dared the horrible impudence of squeaking in its rodent's voice, "Yes."

Magtwilla tilted her head, skewing her left ear to the side. She knew the mouse wasn't her kitten. Or a kitten at all. At least, certainly not a healthy, beautiful one. She remembered Twillatha hunting this very rodent, and, somehow, that connection to her kittens was enough.

Magtwilla stretched out, relaxing for the first time since Magtori left. If this deformed rodent of a kitten meant to be hers, then it would need bathing.

The mouse thought he would die of fear as Magtwilla's sharp tooth-filled mouth approached him, but it was a warm, rough tongue that he felt. Not the points of her teeth. She bathed him thoroughly, and watched him eat. When he'd had his fill, before the mouse could skitter away, Magtwilla bit him gently at the nape of his neck. She carried him with her mouth to her favorite sock drawer where she performed the secret ceremony for naming a new kitten.

This was a kitten she could keep hidden from Todd. This was a kitten she could keep. And as they slept together, predator and prey side-by-side, the mouse willed his heart to stop racing. This dangerous foster mother could eat him whole in one bite, if her heart ever healed and she regained her mind. However, she could keep his belly full of good food until then, and he didn't mind her calling him Twill-tori. Even if it wasn't his true name.

11

COLD TAIL AND THE EYES

ONE DAY, Mama Cat didn't come back to her nest under the porch. She didn't bring warm mice, freshly caught, for Gray Tail and his brothers to eat. She didn't wash their faces and scold them for scuffling. She didn't settle down, all warm on her side, for them to cuddle up next to. She simply wasn't there at all.

Gray Tail was hungry and his brothers cried. One by one, his brother kittens left the nest, venturing out of the safe, enclosed, darkness and into the wide, open, brightness.

They didn't come back either.

Gray Tail was left alone and hungry.

He tried to outwait the hunger, but it grew instead of going away. If the hunger wouldn't leave, then Gray Tail would have to.

Cautiously, Gray Tail crept out from under the wooden slats of the porch. He flattened his tabby body against the ground, creeping so slowly that he didn't make a sound. No one watching would even see him move.

Gray Tail didn't know who he was hiding from— whoever had taken Mama Cat and his brothers, he supposed. Unfortunately, the metal cage that waited for Gray Tail on the other side of the opening under the porch didn't need to hear him or see him move. No matter how slowly he lowered his paw onto the catch, when his weight shifted, the trap snapped shut.

Terror, yowling, hissing, and rattling the cage.

Pink hands came, lifted the metal cage, and carried it, swinging, through the air. The light changed from raw white to curdled gold. Gray Tail had never been inside a human house before—only under one.

The pink hands pulled Gray Tail out of the cage. He scratched them several times, before they wrapped him tightly in a rough, blue towel.

"Poor Kitty," the owner of the pink hands sang, cooing to Gray Tail.

The hands stroked him and molested his ears. He didn't want the hands to touch him.

"I didn't think you'd ever come out."

When the hands finally set Gray Tail free, he darted for the nearest dark corner he could see—an open cupboard under a sink. His brothers were there! And a bowl of food! Gray Tail bumped his head against his brothers—all three of them—and then he settled down to eat, purring much too loudly for happiness. His purrs were frantic, desperate. *Let me be safe; let me be warm; let me be.*

The hands did not let Gray Tail be. Each kitten by turns was pulled out from the cupboard, wrapped in a towel, scritched, and bothered daily. Sometimes, the towel was loosened, but Gray Tail learned that if he used the opportunity to scratch and bite the hands, the towel would be rewrapped too tightly for him to move.

Gray Tail learned not to scratch and bite.

But he didn't learn not to hate.

He hated the hands—their pinkness, their wiggling, scritching, and the cooing voice that came with them: "Such a pretty kitty! So much calmer than your brothers!"

Gray Tail's brothers didn't hate the hands. They pressed their heads against the scritches, arched their backs, and bared their bellies. They relaxed and let their guard down. So, of course, the hands made each of them disappear.

"I've found homes for your brothers, Simon. And my mother says that your Mama Cat is taming nicely," the voice of the hands said. "But, you're so shy, I think you should stay here with me."

Gray Tail lived in the house, avoiding the hands who called him Simon. He slept under the couch, hid behind the washing machine, and only came out to sit on window sills when he knew the hands were gone.

"Simon?" the hands called. "Kitty, kitty?"

Gray Tail refused the shiny objects and fish-smelling treats that the hands dangled for him. He would not be lured out from his safety. He could forage for himself—when the hands were gone, he always found bowls of food waiting for him. He didn't need the hands. He didn't need their barbed charity.

Gray Tail learned the borders of his cage well. The windows showed him a world free from the tyranny of the hands, but he could not get there.

Then, one day, the hands brought out a plastic and metal box that reminded Gray Tail of the cage they'd use to trap him before. He didn't know what new horror might lie on the other side of this new cage, but he didn't want to. His fur fluffed; his back arched; he hissed.

"Easy now, Simon. I'm just going to take you to my mother's house. She has your Mama Cat and two of your brothers. I thought you might be happier there. You're clearly not happy here."

Gray Tail didn't understand the voice of the hands, but he hated it when they said *Simon*. He ran for the couch.

But the hands followed him to the couch, carried there by stomping feet. The couch flew upward, revealing Gray Tail. He ran and hid again, but the stomping feet followed him. Every piece of furniture moved at the behest of the hands. Nowhere was safe. Finally, cornered behind the washing machine, Gray Tail had no choice. The hands came at him, and he abandoned his training—he scratched and bit, fighting for his life.

The voice of the hands screamed, and Gray Tail smelled blood in the air. He cowered behind the washing machine, his last line of defense, and listened to the voice of the hands.

"I'm sorry, Simon," the voice said. "I did my best."

When he came out from behind the washing machine, hours later, the door to the washing room was closed, but one of the windows was open. Cold air blew in, fresh from outside.

Gray Tail had never felt more triumphant than when he jumped through that open window.

Outside was filled with exciting, skittering creatures— bugs and mice and squirrels and birds. Gray Tail knew how to catch none of them. He had to live on the same sorts of bowls of food he'd scrounged for himself inside the house of the hands—they appeared out here too; once a day, beside the door to the hands' house.

But Gray Tail watched the tantalizing creatures. He chased squirrels and pounced on spiders. He chewed on sour grasses and sweet flowers. He slept in sunlight, unfiltered through glass. He ranged through the neighborhood, free and unfettered. Except, of course, for his need to return for the daily bowl of food.

The weather turned. Sunlight was still bright, but it didn't warm Gray Tail like it used to. Then, day by day, the sunlight went away—the sun barely rose, and clouds obscured its brilliance. Everything was dark and cold. Snow fell. Rain followed, covering the trees and snow in ice.

Gray Tail shivered in the abandoned nest under the porch and ignored the voice of the hands calling, "Simon? Kitty, kitty?"

Gray Tail shivered, shielded from the snow and ice, waiting for the cold to leave. But like his hunger had grown, the cold grew. It held him tightly; it held him still, like the blue towel that the hands had wrapped around him. The cold grew until it was bigger than him. It grew until he stopped shivering.

Gray Tail dreamed that the earth opened up beneath him. It cracked wide, and he plummeted down into the dark. He landed on paws that were still numb with cold but burned at the touch of the ground. He heard cats crying in the distance.

A chimera approached from the flickering shadows—it had the body of a cat, but instead of a single cat's head on its shoulders, three strange heads sprouted—one like Mama Cat's, a second like a mouse's with teasing laughter in its eyes, and the third was a giant pink hand.

The chimera spoke to him with its cat head: "Cold Tail, this is your ninth life. You cannot be reborn, so you must choose where your soul will dwell." The cat head looked over its shoulder toward the flickering shadows where cats cried. "Will you be Gray Tail? Ungrateful and feral?"

Gray Tail stepped toward the shadows, but each step burned his numb paws worse. He smelled fire, and his whiskers sizzled as if the very air singed them. In the shadows, he saw the crying cats writhe and twist. Their bodies moved unnaturally, vaguely cat-shaped but broken. Giant mice stood over them, jabbing the cats with spears and tridents.

"Or can you be tamed?" The pink hand sprouting hideously from the chimera's shoulders pointed behind Gray Tail.

Gray Tail looked that way, but all he saw was a path leading into darkness.

"Until you choose, you will remain in purgatory," the chimera squeaked with its mouse head, "You will be Cold Tail." The mouse head laughed, cackling evilly.

The earth shook under Gray Tail's paws. He turned and fled toward the path, away from the crying cats, away from the chimera, and away from his choice.

Gray Tail awoke in his nest under the porch, colder than ever. He roused his stiff limbs, stretched, and paced restlessly under the porch. The ice and snow made him feel trapped. He had to leave. He had to be free.

Gray Tail came out from under the porch. He walked over the snow, stepping so lightly his paws left no prints. He wandered the neighborhood, enjoying his freedom, even though the cold gnawed at him.

When he returned to the house of the hands, Gray Tail found that the bowl of food by the door held no appeal. Neither did the dead mice he found, frozen by the ice storm.

Gray Tail ate no more.

When the snow thawed, his paws left no tracks in the slush and mud. He didn't bother squeezing through the hole to his nest under the porch any more; he could walk right through the planks.

When the sun shone on Gray Tail, it didn't warm him. It didn't touch him at all. It passed right through him, and he cast no shadow.

Days and weeks passed; the days grew longer; but Gray Tail never grew warmer.

Sometimes in his dreams, Gray Tail felt a burning in his paws and smelled fire. He heard the broken cats crying for him to join them. But he held still until he awoke again, cold but free. He wanted nothing of the warmth of hell.

The only other time that Gray Tail felt warm was when the voice of the hands called to him: "Simon! Here kitty! Simon!"

The name was like a tether to his heart, tugging him to come closer. It fought against the fear and hate, warring to melt the cold that filled his ghostly, incorporeal cat form.

Gray Tail wouldn't go to the hands, but he began to watch them. He skulked outside the windows of their house. He watched them hold books, carry plates of food, fold clothes, and brush the hair away from the face that said his name. "Simon."

He hid in the bushes when the hands came to the front door and called to him, holding a bowl of food. When the hands gave up calling, "Here kitty, kitty!", they left the bowl of food lying on the ground. They went back inside and closed the door.

Gray Tail crept out of the bushes, came up to the bowl, and sniffed the food. He wasn't hungry, but the smell of the food felt warm in his belly.

He decided to follow the hands inside. He walked right through the closed front door.

Gray Tail had never entered the house of the hands by his own free will before. It looked different to him, knowing that he could leave by any path, none of the walls could hold him. But they could hide him. The hands still scared him, so Gray Tail kept his distance, following them from room to room, hidden inside the walls.

When the hands lay down to sleep that night, Gray Tail came out of the wall and jumped onto the bed. His weightless paws made no indentation in the covers, but his presence wafted over the body of the hands like a cool breeze. The hands pulled the covers tighter.

Gray Tail crouched beside the head of the hands and watched its slow breathing and the flickering of its eyes. He'd never looked at the face that called him "Simon" before. It was pink and naked, oval and knobby. Completely unlike Mama Cat's face. But it had eyes.

When the eyes opened in the morning, they were brown and warm. Gray Tail was so busy looking at them, he didn't notice the hands moving, rearranging the blankets. One of the hands passed right through him. It burned like fire.

Gray Tail startled and jumped off of the bed. He watched the hands move around the room, opening drawers, taking out clothes, fixing the bed. For the first time, he also watched the brown eyes. They didn't look at him. They looked at the hands, mostly.

Gray Tail hid in the bedroom wall until the hands left the house for the day, but he didn't leave the house. It was warmer inside.

When the hands and eyes came home that night, Gray Tail followed them more boldly from room to room. He began to hope that the the eyes would see him. He wanted to be looked at. He wanted to feel real and acknowledged, no longer a cold shadow, a mere ghost of a cat.

The hands cooked dinner. They chopped onions, peeled potatoes, and fried a fish. The fish smelled sweet, but the only hunger in Gray Tail's belly was for the warmth he remembered seeing in the hands' brown eyes that morning.

After dinner, the hands carried a bowl of food to the front door, and the voice called for him. "Simon! Simon!" The eyes scanned the darkness outside, but they didn't look down at Gray Tail, weaving between the hands' feet, as if he could rub up against them. He could not, but he could walk through them. When he did, the hands put the food bowl down. The voice said, "Brr. It's cold tonight."

The hands and eyes went back inside.

Too late, he'd learned to see the hands for what they really were—generosity, companionship, and warmth. He saw the eyes now, but the eyes did not see him.

Gray Tail cried, a sad meowl, a haunting sound that carried across the ethereal planes separating him from the living world. His cry said that he was ready to choose, ready to change, ready to be Simon.

His cry called the hands back to the door, and when the hands opened the door, the eyes looked down. Brown eyes saw the shadowy, translucent figure of a gray tabby.

"Simon?"

Gray Tail meowed and wove between the hands' feet again. The hands stood there for a long time before moving, but then the hands came down and reached to touch Gray Tail. He didn't shrink away. The hands were warm where they passed through his body, and he wondered how he had ever hated them.

Gray Tail followed the hands inside the house, purring, and jumped onto their lap when they sat down to hold a book. He curled up, feeling safe. Finally, all the cold melted out of Gray Tail. He fell asleep and dreamed that his eyes,

Mama Cat's eyes, and the brown eyes of the hands all turned into stars and rose into the sky. The six stars—and many more—locked into a perfect constellation, always seeing each other, never alone, forever above the fire and cold on the mortal plane.

12

ALL THE CATS OF THE RAINBOW

SARAH WAS one of three dozen kittens who all lived in a cozy garage that had been retro-fitted into the perfect Persian cat playground. Scratching posts and cat toys littered the floor. The walls were a veritable maze of carpeted shelving— perfect for perching. Sarah ran wild with her sisters, brothers, litters worth of cousins, four aunts, mother, and grandmother. They were all fluffy, white, purebred fuzzballs just like her. She felt safe and loved.

The human they called Master brought Sarah and her family food and scritches, lots of brushing, every day. One day, Master brought a new human with him. She sat on the floor and whipped a string about, wriggling it like a snake. "I'm looking for a playful kitten," she said. "I want a cat that will be good for my five-year-old nephew."

"They're all playful at this age," Master said.

Sarah and several of her cousins chased the string, tumbling over each other and themselves, trying to trap it against the floor with their claws.

"But I think that one," Master pointed at Sarah, "has a

particularly friendly personality. I call her Sarah. She'd be good for a child."

The new human dropped the string. Sarah's cousins lost interest and scurried off. Sarah continued clawing and chewing at it until the new human picked her up. She held Sarah with two hands, flat Persian muzzle only inches from her own face.

Sarah looked the human right in the eye and meowed to be put down. She had a string to catch!

The human laughed and said, "Perfect."

The humans moved to a table in the corner of the garage where they signed and traded pieces of paper. Sarah lost interest in them and their boring human ways. Her mother, however, had had litters before. She knew what was coming, and she came to Sarah, washed her face, and purred at her to tell her it would be okay. It was the start of an adventure, the start of a new life.

The new human put Sarah in a cat carrier with a squeaky yellow mouse toy and a bunched up towel. It smelled warm and fresh. It was comfortable and different. Sarah felt like she was hiding, and hiding was fun.

"We're going to a birthday party," the human said as she placed the closed carrier onto the passenger seat of her car. "And you're the guest of honor." She got into the car herself and started it up. "We just have to stop at my lab on the way. I left an experiment running that I need to check on. I'm a scientist. Oh, god, I'm explaining myself to my nephew's cat..."

The human stopped talking, and Sarah got tired of hiding. She scrabbled at the door of the carrier, but it didn't open. She meowed that she wanted to go home. She meowed it again and again. Finally the car stopped. The human got out and brought the carrier with her.

"Why won't you stop meowing? Look, I just need a minute to check on the optics."

The human set down the closed carrier and left it on the floor. Sarah stopped meowing, but she kept scrabbling at the door of the carrier. It must not have been fully latched, because she managed to pry it open.

Sarah peeked out, but she wasn't greeted by the friendly nose of one of her cousins. She stepped out of the carrier and into the scientist's lab. She looked all around, but she didn't see any cats anywhere.

No sisters. No brothers. No cousins, aunts, or grand-mother. Not even a mama. No other cats at all.

That wasn't quite true. Sarah realized that she did see a cat—or the shape of a cat, sleeping on a pile of books on a lab table. It was a high table, but Sarah jumped up to see the cat better.

He was an orange tabby, but half of the time Sarah could see right through him. It was as if he wasn't there, and he was there, at the same time.

"Who are you?" Sarah meowed.

The orange tabby lifted his head and looked at her with golden eyes. At the same time, he lay still, continuing to sleep. It was as if Sarah was seeing two cats occupying the same space. They overlapped and faded into each other, looking clear and strong together, but faded and transparent when they moved apart.

"I'm Fred, the lab cat," the orange tabby said. He also didn't say it, instead rolling over and yawning.

Sarah blinked, confused. Yet, no matter how strange Fred seemed, he was more like her mama cat than anything else in this strange place. "Why are you... both?" Sarah asked.

"One of the scientist's experiments," Fred said. "I got

caught in it." He washed a paw, meticulously cleaning his claws. "Something about boxes and double slits. Now I can sleep and not sleep at the same time." The sleeping version of Fred cracked open an eye and hissed at Sarah, "Are you still here? Go away!"

Sarah had been hissed at before. She had lots of cousins. It didn't faze her. "There aren't enough cats here," she said. "Only you—or the two of you—and me. Will you be my mama?" She purred hopefully and stepped toward the double tabby.

Fred rolled his eyes and said, politely, "No." He also swatted a paw towards her, claws out, hissing, "I said, go away!"

Sarah didn't quite know if Fred was there or not—would his claws scratch her or pass right through? She played it safe and ran, dashing haphazardly along the lab table. When she reached the end, she jumped to the next.

"Hey, kitten!" the scientist yelled, noticing the little escape artist. "Get away from that prism!"

Sarah flattened her ears at the sound of the scientist's raised voice. Master had never yelled. She didn't like this new human or her strange cat. Sarah ran away from both of them.

She ran straight into the half-meter tall, rhomboid, crystal prism that the scientist was yelling about. Sarah saw her own flat Persian face reflected in the prism as it toppled out of its jerry-rigged base. Laser light scattered in every direction, and Sarah felt herself pulling apart, stretching out. The smell of ionization and singed cat fur filled the air.

But Sarah was okay.

All seven of her.

Fred laughed. He also looked away in disgust. He hadn't wanted to share his role as lab cat with a single white puff-ball. He certainly didn't want to share with red, orange, yellow, green, blue, indigo, and violet ones.

A harmony of meows—higher pitched from Violet, Blue, and Indigo; subtly lower from Red—expressed surprise and confusion. All seven of Sarah looked at each other with wide green eyes, unchanged by the prism. On Green, her eyes and fur matched perfectly, a solid emerald kitten. On Red, her sparkling green eyes framed by ruddy red fur gave her face a Christmas look.

Red flopped onto her side, feeling slow and languid. Orange flopped down beside her. They bathed each others' ears, a strangely intimate sensation, more so than bathing the ears of a cousin.

Violet, Blue, and Indigo practically vibrated with excitement and began chasing each other, mewing in delight at playing kittens' games again. Except this time, there was no fighting, no compromise like with her litter mates. Violet, Blue, and Indigo were all Sarah, and they all wanted to play the same game.

Yellow, followed by Green, cautiously approached Fred. He was still the closest thing to a mama cat around. "What happened to me?" she meowed. Green's voice echoed hers, a perfect copy cat.

"Science," Fred meowed, one of him with a sneer and the other with reverence.

"Don't get used to this," the scientist said, scooping Red and Orange up. They were too lazy to run. "My sister would kill me if I gave her son *seven* kittens." It took longer to catch Violet, Blue, and Indigo as they skittered around the legs of the lab table. Yellow and Green tried to cower behind Fred, but he had no interest in shielding them.

Soon the seven kittens of the rainbow found themselves

dumped together into a cardboard box, their brightly colored fur mashed against each other.

"That should hold you while I reverse the setup," the scientist said.

All seven of Sarah heard the scientist messing with her lab equipment. Several of her squirmed; the others lazed together, calm and accepting. Yet, they all felt warm and cozy so close together.

"I hope this works... The last thing I need is to multiply seven kittens into forty-nine."

The scientist picked up the box of Sarah. Claws dug into the tilting cardboard, but it was too smooth to get a good purchase. The seven kittens slid out and landed in a pile next to the rhomboid prism again. Violet, Indigo, and Blue tensed their muscles to pounce away, but they weren't fast enough.

The laser light hit them, shining from every direction. All seven kittens squeezed closer together, fusing into one space. Fusing into one kitten.

The buzz of electronics powering down. The zip of lasers turning off. Sarah's mouth felt dry and coppery. Her white fur fluffed with static electricity. She jumped, startled.

There was only one of her.

"That's better," the scientist said. Human hands grabbed Sarah around her fluffy white middle. "Now, back in the carrier for you."

Through the metal grated door of the carrier, now properly latched shut, Sarah saw Fred, still lying on a lab table. "Goodbye, Rainbow Cat," one of him said. The other winked. Apparently, he felt more charitable toward a kitten who was *leaving*.

This time, Sarah settled into the rumpled towels, folded her paws beneath her, and waited quietly through the car ride. Her mind felt noisy, filled with the memory of all the different kittens she'd been. She felt lazy and energetic, curious and bored all at once.

"No more meowing?" the scientist asked. "I guess you got quite a scare back there. I probably should have learned my lesson about cats in the lab with Fred."

The car stopped. The scientist got out and brought the carrier with her. Sarah heard shrieking and giggling— higher pitched human voices than she'd ever heard before.

"Aunt Carrie, what is that! Is it my present?"

"Hold on, Toby. Let me take her out." The scientist opened the grated metal door and lifted Sarah out. A single pair of green cat eyes looked over the scene—children in paper hats, streamers hung tantalizingly from the ceiling, and toys everywhere. It was complete chaos. It was exciting.

The memory of her violet, blue, and indigo selves tensed, ready to skitter and leap at the dangling streamers. The part of Sarah that had been red and orange wanted to laze on the floor, batting idly at one of the plush toys. The rest of her stared wide-eyed at the children.

One of the children, a boy with a hat shaped like a plush birthday cake complete with cartoony candles on his head stepped forward. "Oh, Auntie, she's beautiful." His brown eyes were wide with wonder, just like Sarah's green ones.

"Her name is Sarah."

The scientist handed the little bundle of white fluff to Toby. His hands were small and squeezed, but Sarah wriggled until he held her better.

"Sarah's a boring name," Toby said.

"Okay," the scientist said. "How about Rainbow?"

Toby grinned. "Yeah."

"She needs a hat!" one of the other children declared.

Toby shifted Sarah, now Rainbow, into the crook of his

arm, grabbed a paper hat, and placed it over her ears. Rainbow's flat white muzzle frowned, but she opened her mouth and gnawed on the paper hat's string. Toby laughed. His delight more than made up for the indignity of the hat.

Rainbow purred. All of her.

For the rest of the afternoon, Rainbow was handed from one child to another, dressed in doll clothes despite protestation, and tempted with strings. She didn't miss her cousins and littermates at all. The children kept her plenty busy, and she could still feel all the different colors inside of herself.

When the party was over, Toby took Rainbow up to his room. He put her on the bed, and the sunlight from his window warmed the white fur on her back. The scientist was gone, and Rainbow liked Toby. She decided to trust him with a secret.

She relaxed and let herself drift apart, come unfocused. She'd realized that she could do it again: one white kitten split into seven colorful ones. Seven pairs of green eyes stared at Toby from a rainbow of kitten faces.

"Oh wow," he said with the widest grin. "We are going to have so much fun."

Sarah focused herself and fused back together, all of her wanting to nap in the sunlight while Toby petted her.

She was one cat, but one cat could be many.

13

IN A CAT'S EYES

JASON's brushy tail wagged like a flag as he trotted down the sidewalk in front of his house. He strained his neck against the leash, just a little, to help his master out. His master was always reluctant to go on walks, and the only explanation Jason could think of was that she must tire out easily. Heaven knew, Jason had energy to spare, so it was only fair that he help pull her along.

Inside the house, Jason's master unclipped his leash, freeing the Collie pup of boundless energy to run from room to room until he found Myra, the aged Siamese cat.

"Myra!" he barked when he found her sitting in a windowsill. "I just went on another walk!"

Myra's dark ears flattened, trying vainly to shut out the clamor of Jason's barking.

"There were squirrels! And ducks! And I almost made it into the lake today, but the master's feet seemed to get stuck, and she got so heavy, I just couldn't pull her into the water!"

Blue eyes glared at Jason.

"Don't worry," he barked, "I'm sure I'll pull her into the water tomorrow."

The eyes kept glaring.

Jason felt compelled to make Myra understand how wonderful his walk had been, so he jumped his front paws up onto the windowsill beside her, bringing his nose into swatting range. Myra swatted him.

"What was that for!" Jason barked. "I was just trying to get close enough that you'd be able to hear me tell you about the squirrels and ducks!"

A sound rose in Myra's throat—low and sinister—that made Jason's nerves jangle. "I don't care about squirrels and ducks," she hissed. "Leave me alone."

Jason couldn't believe that. Of course, Myra cared about squirrels and ducks. How could she not? They were so exciting when they ran away from him! Maybe he hadn't explained them well enough. Or... Well, the more Jason thought about it, maybe explaining squirrels and ducks wasn't really enough. Maybe, one had to actually see them. Oneself.

"Do you ever get to go on walks?" Jason barked.

Myra skewed one of her ears and stared at Jason scornfully. She didn't need to answer that question. They lived in the same house, day in and day out. He went on a walk every day. Sometimes their master took him to the beach. Myra slept on the sofa and the windowsill and behind the washing machine. She was in the house when he left on his walks. She was in the house when he came back. She was an indoor-only cat.

"Oh, I'm sorry, Myra," Jason barked. He'd never thought before about what it would be like to miss out on chasing squirrels and ducks, meeting other dogs on their walks, and splashing in the ocean surf. Suddenly, Myra's life looked very small to him.

In his moment of sympathy for her, Jason looked up into

Myra's blue eyes and saw the room they stood in reflected in miniature. He saw himself, brown eyes and bushy brown fur, looking sad and concerned staring back from inside the confines of that little world. But, as he stared, he felt himself drawn in deeper, down into the tiny, reflected world inside those blue eyes.

Inside Myra's eyes, the glass panels of the windows behind her melted away, becoming portals to a magical realm. In that realm, squirrels and ducks didn't run from her. They chittered and squawked in languages Jason had heard before but never understood. The squirrels brought her gifts of nuts and berries, and the ducks fanned her with their wings, calling her a queen. They held dances in her honor. All night long, the ducks and squirrels whirled and twirled together in the shimmering moonlight beside the lake.

Myra lived years among them, longer than Jason would live in a lifetime, and when she died, her life would only be a tiny part of the great string of lifetimes she would live— each life a pearl on a necklace worn by a great goddess cat Jason had never imagined. A cat who's ears were black holes and eyes were stars. Her whiskers were gossamer nebulae.

Jason glimpsed snatches of Myra's other lives:

—*a black cat sniffing a bubbling cauldron as a woman poured potions into it and chanted*—

—*a great striped tiger, running through the dappled light of a jungle*—

—*a giant beast with a whiskered face, a sinuous spine, dozens of legs, and wings that blotted out the sky*—

—*a brown dog, an overgrown puppy really, barking uselessly at a Siamese cat he loved but didn't understand...*

Oh! That was Jason. And in that moment of infinite regression, Jason felt himself falling into himself and into himself, over and over again, through the double mirror of his own and Myra's eyes. There were depths inside those feline eyes that Jason had never imagined.

Then Myra looked away, breaking the spell and snapping Jason back into himself. She turned her pale blue eyes toward the glass wall of the windowpane, an impenetrable barrier to her frail, cat's body.

Jason watched her, stunned into silence, for once. She could not follow him into the world outside their house. But she had worlds inside her that he could only barely begin to smell.

ABOUT THE AUTHOR

Mary E. Lowd is a prolific science-fiction and furry writer in Oregon. She's had more than 200 short stories and a dozen novels published, always with more on the way. Her work has won four Ursa Major Awards, ten Leo Literary Awards, and four Cóyotl Awards. She edited FurPlanet's ROAR anthology series for five years, and she is now the editor and founder of the furry e-zine *Zooscape*. She lives in a crashed spaceship, disguised as a house and hidden behind a rose garden, with an extensive menagerie of animals, some real and some imaginary.

For more information:
marylowd.com

To read Mary's short stories:
deepskyanchor.com

For news, updates, discounts, and deals:
marylowd.com/newsletter

ALSO BY MARY E. LOWD

Otters In Space

Otters In Space

Otters In Space 2: Jupiter, Deadly

Otters In Space 3: Octopus Ascending

Otters In Space 4: First Moustronaut

Otters In Space Spinoffs

In a Dog's World

When A Cat Loves A Dog

Jove Deadly's Lunar Detective Agency (with Garrett Marco)

The Entangled Universe

Entanglement Bound

The Entropy Fountain

Starwhal in Flight

Entangled Universe Spinoffs

You're Cordially Invited to Crossroads Station

Welcome to Wespirtech

Beyond Wespirtech

Brunch at the All Alien Cafe

Xeno-Spectre

Hell Moon

The Ancient Egg

The Celestial Fragments (A Labyrinth of Souls Trilogy)

The Snake's Song

The Bee's Waltz

The Otter's Wings

Tri-Galactic Trek

Tri-Galactic Trek

Nexus Nine: A Tri-Galactic Trek Novel

Voyage of the Wanderlust: A Tri-Galactic Trek Novel

Commander Annie and Other Adventures

The Necromouser and Other Magical Cats

The Opposite of Memory

Queen Hazel and Beloved Beverly

Some Words Burn Brightly: An Illuminated Collection of Poetry

Furry Fiction Is Everywhere (with Ian Madison Keller)